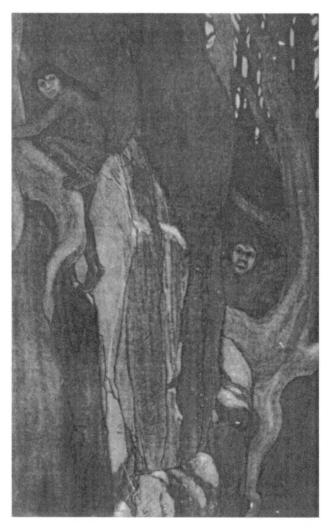

"I pursued her from tree to tree."

BEFORE ADAM

BY

JACK LONDON

WITH NUMEROUS ILLUSTRATIONS BY

CHARLES LIVINGSTON BULL

Introduction to the Bison Books Edition by
Dennis L. McKiernan

EPILOGUE BY LOREN EISELEY

UNIVERSITY OF NEBRASKA PRESS
LINCOLN AND LONDON

"Epilogue" by Loren Eiseley is reprinted with the permission of Simon & Schuster from *Before Adam* by Jack London. Copyright © 1962 by Macmillan Publishing Company.
Introduction and Listing of Peoples and Characters © 2000 by the University of Nebraska Press

☻

First Bison Books printing: 2000

Library of Congress Cataloging-in-Publication Data
London, Jack, 1876–1916.
Before Adam / Jack London; introduction to the Bison Books edition by Dennis L. McKiernan; epilogue by Loren Eiseley.—Commemorative ed.
p. cm.—(Bison frontiers of imagination)
ISBN 0-8032-7993-0 (pbk.: alk. paper)
1. Man, Prehistoric—Fiction. 2. Dreams—Fiction.
I. Title. II. Series.
PS3523.O46B4 2000
813'.52—dc21
99-054898

" THESE are our ancestors, and their history is our history. Remember that as surely as we one day swung down out of the trees and walked upright, just as surely, on a far earlier day, did we crawl up out of the sea and achieve our first adventure on land."

CONTENTS

INTRODUCTION

Dennis L. McKiernan

At the time Jack London wrote *Before Adam*,[1] the evidence supporting the evolution of humans was meager (and quite controversial). Nevertheless, he relied on what there was (or some of it) to fashion his story. In those early days of the 1900s, many held a general belief that humanity had evolved from apes—the so-called missing link theory, hypothesized by some who followed Darwin—although no confirming fossil had been found to support such an idea. Of course, they had it wrong, for both humans and apes evolved from a common ancestor. Any "missing link" existed farther down the limb of the evolutionary tree, somewhat before the two genera diverged along their separate primate branches. One of these branches led to several different offshoots of hominids, and one of the offshoots ultimately culminated in *Homo sapiens sapiens* (modern humankind). The other primate branch led to the various offshoots of apekind, or so the current anthropological findings indicate.

Given where hominid fossils have been found, the evidence shows that more than one wave of the evolving primitive forms of humans—protohominids—spread out from Africa and across the world. Evidence also indicates that one wave may have emerged from southeast Asia, and some think that the Middle East may have been the cradle of some branches of humankind.

But guess what? Even though London didn't have the evidence of the many different hominid fossils subsequently discovered (such as the bones of Lucy), nor the mitochondrial studies (which led to the somewhat questionable "Eve" hypothesis), nor the fossilized 3.5-million-year-old hominid footprints showing that upright walking occurred long past, nor the evidence of separate migratory waves of humans' evolutionary ancestors coming out of Africa, nor other such findings, he may have gotten some things right. You see, in London's tale *Before Adam* at least two kinds of hominids interact. One set is caught on its evolutionary branch at a point where an entire folk are more or less like the chimpanzees over on their separate primate branch, though they are one evolutionary step above those anthropoids. Perhaps the folk of the tale are similar to *Homo erectus* (Java man: *Pithecanthropus*). The second set of hominids uses speech, fire, bows and arrows, and other tools. Perhaps London was thinking of Neanderthals for their model, though various means of dating the fossil record indicate that Neanderthals are a relatively recent species that may not have used language. Or perhaps London thought the fire-users were Cro-Magnons, though they are more recent still.

Nevertheless, by making use of two separate hominid species in his story, London showed that he did not subscribe to the single "missing-link" postulate popular in his time. He instead drew parallel (but time-disjointed, it seems) evolutionary paths for the development of humanity and apes.

You might think that this tale would have as its protagonists the folk of the latter species (the ones with speech, fire, and so forth), but London chose instead to feature those hominids that were just a step above the level of the chimpanzee. By doing so, he took the harder tack, one that required greater imagination and story-telling powers to make the protagonists sympathetic. But London always did choose to tell tales in which individuals cling to life by their fingernails and strive against elemental furies and savage cruelties. In this tale the beings of little skill and mental capacities face far greater odds than those with greater capabilities against such a brutal world. And so he tells the story of a barely above ape near-man, and it is one heckuva tale, one that rightfully can be called a truly splendid fantasy.

What's that? you ask. Jack London? The man who wrote *White Fang, Call of the Wild,* and *The Sea-Wolf? That* Jack London? He wrote *fantasy?*

Yes, that Jack London.

Granted, those three novels—*White Fang, Call of the Wild,* and *The Sea-Wolf*—are the ones best remembered, but London was a much more prolific writer than most of us know, and his subjects ranged far and wide. He wrote twenty-one novels and seventeen *collections* of short stories as well as quite a few more short stories not in collections to date; additionally, he wrote essays, a play, and a number of nonfiction works (at least five, though the list is incomplete).[2] His tales took form in many genres, fantasy not the least of them.

As you can see, even though he died of kidney disease at the age of forty (before he reached his prime, I believe), he was undeniably prolific, a man well suited to the credo attributed to him:

I would rather be ashes than dust!
I would rather that my spark should burn out in a blaze than it should be stifled by dry rot.
I would rather be a superb meteor, every atom of me in magnificent glow, than a sleepy and permanent planet.
The function of man is to live, not to exist.
I shall not waste my days trying to prolong them.
I shall use my time.

Following that credo, London produced a magnificent body of work. Even if the only thing he had written had been the tale *Before Adam*, it alone would have been a splendid solo. As a fantasy, it tells the tale of a modern man who, in his vivid dreams, dredges up ancestral memories of a verge-of-human, prehistoric life lived at the evolutionary dawn of humankind, a life lived as "Big-Tooth," a prehistoric child and then man who was neither fully human nor ape but something in between. It is the story of a being on the cusp of evolutionary change, when—for Big-Tooth's hominid branch—language was just beginning, the mastery of fire was yet to be learned, and his society was yet partially arboreal. It is a great adventure: a modern man telling a tale about when he was a prehistoric near-man, one of those who came before Adam.

So, sit back and abandon your disbelief, set aside the latest anthropological findings, take up this book, and prepare to enjoy, for after all, 'tis Jack London telling this tale.

NOTES

1. First serialized in *Everybody's Magazine,* October 1906–February 1907.

2. Information about London's lesser-known works is available on the Internet at the many sites dedicated to Jack London. One such site is <http://sunsite.berkeley.edu/London/>, and it contains information not only about London but about some of his writings. It also supplies links to other Jack London sites.

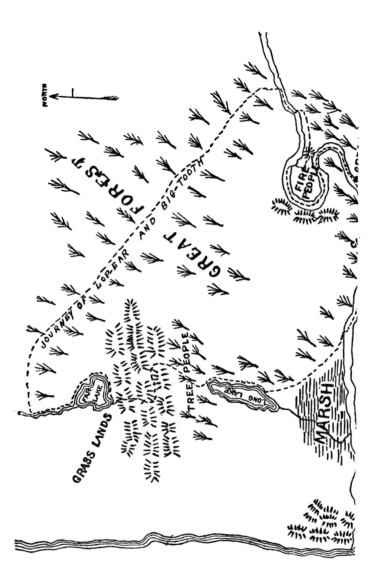

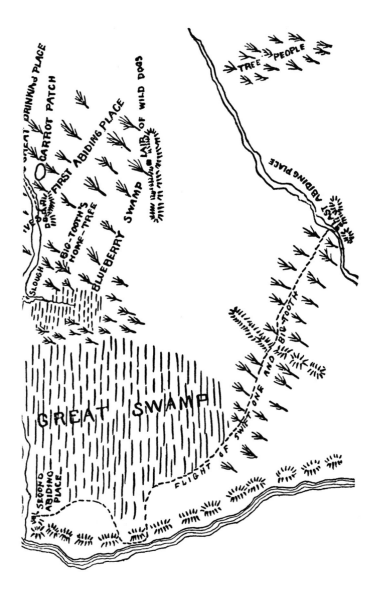

CHAPTER I

PICTURES! Pictures! Pictures! Often, before I learned, did I wonder whence came the multitudes of pictures that thronged my dreams; for they were pictures the like of which I had never seen in real wake-a-day life. They tormented my childhood, making of my dreams a procession of nightmares and a little later convincing me that I was different from my kind, a creature unnatural and accursed.

In my days only did I attain any measure of happiness. My nights marked the reign of fear — and such fear! I make bold to state that no man of all the men who walk the earth with me ever suffer fear of like kind and degree. For my fear is the fear of long ago, the fear that was rampant in the Younger World, and in the youth of the Younger World. In short, the fear that reigned supreme in that period known as the Mid-Pleistocene.

What do I mean? I see explanation is necessary before I can tell you of the substance of my dreams. Otherwise, little could you know of the meaning of the things I know so well. As I write this, all the beings and happenings of that other world rise up before me in vast phantasmagoria, and I know that to you they would be rhymeless and reasonless.

What to you the friendship of Lop-Ear, the warm lure of the Swift One, the lust and the atavism of Red-Eye? A screaming incoherence and no more. And a screaming incoherence, likewise, the doings of the Fire People and the Tree People, and the gibbering councils of the horde. For you know not the peace of the cool caves in the cliffs, the circus of the drinking-places at the end of the day. You have never felt the bite of the morning wind in the tree-tops, nor is the taste of young bark sweet in your mouth.

It would be better, I dare say, for you to make your approach, as I made mine, through my childhood. As a boy I was very like other boys — in my waking hours. It was in my sleep that I was different. From my earliest recollection my sleep was a period of terror. Rarely were my dreams tinctured with happiness. As a rule, they were stuffed with fear — and with a fear so strange and alien that it had no ponderable quality. No fear that I experienced in my waking life resembled the fear that possessed me in my sleep. It was of a quality and kind that transcended all my experiences.

For instance, I was a city boy, a city child, rather, to whom the country was an unexplored domain. Yet I never dreamed of cities; nor did a house ever occur in any of my dreams. Nor, for that matter, did any of my human kind ever break through the wall of my sleep. I, who had seen trees only in parks and illustrated books, wandered in my sleep through interminable forests. And further, these dream trees were not a mere blur on my vision. They were sharp and distinct. I was on terms of practised intimacy with them. I saw every branch and twig; I saw and knew every different leaf. Well do I remember the first time in my waking life that I saw an oak tree. As I looked at the leaves and branches and gnarls, it came to me with distressing vividness that I had seen that same kind of tree many and countless times in my sleep. So I was not surprised, still later on in my life, to recognize instantly, the first time I saw them, trees such as the spruce, the yew, the birch, and the laurel. I had seen them all before, and was seeing them even then, every night, in my sleep.

This, as you have already discerned, violates the first law of dreaming, namely, that in one's dreams one sees only what he has seen in his waking life, or combinations of the things he has seen in his waking life. But all my dreams violated this law. In my dreams I never saw *anything* of which I had knowledge in my waking life. My dream life and my waking life were lives apart, with not one thing in common save myself. I was the connecting link that somehow lived both lives.

Early in my childhood I learned that nuts came from the grocer, berries from the fruit man; but before ever that knowledge was mine, in my dreams I picked nuts from trees, or gathered them and ate them from the ground underneath trees, and in the same way I ate berries from vines and bushes. This was beyond any experience of mine.

I shall never forget the first time I saw blueberries served on the table. I had never seen blueberries before, and yet, at the sight of them, there leaped up in my mind memories of dreams wherein I had wandered through swampy land eating my fill of them. My mother set before me a dish of the berries. I filled my spoon, but before I raised it to my mouth I knew just how they would taste. Nor was I disappointed. It was the same tang that I had tasted a thousand times in my sleep.

Snakes? Long before I had heard of the existence of snakes, I was tormented by them in my sleep. They lurked for me in the forest glades; leaped up, striking, under my feet; squirmed off through the dry grass or across naked patches of rock; or pursued me into the tree-tops, encircling the trunks with their great shining bodies, driving me higher and higher or farther and farther out on swaying and crackling branches, the ground a dizzy distance beneath me. Snakes!—with their forked tongues, their beady eyes and glittering scales, their hissing and their rattling—did I not already know them far too well on that day of my first circus when I saw the snake-charmer lift them up? They were old friends of mine, enemies rather, that peopled my nights with fear.

Ah, those endless forests, and their horror-haunted gloom! For what eternities have I wandered through them, a timid, hunted creature, starting at the least sound, frightened of my own shadow, keyed-up, ever alert and vigilant, ready on the instant to dash away in mad flight for my life. For I was the prey of all manner of fierce life that dwelt in the forest, and it was in ecstasies of fear that I fled before the hunting monsters.

When I was five years old I went to my first circus. I came home from it sick — but not from peanuts and pink lemonade. Let me tell you. As we entered the animal tent, a hoarse roaring shook the air. I tore my hand loose from my father's and dashed wildly back through the entrance. I collided with people, fell down; and all the time I was screaming with terror. My father caught me and soothed me. He pointed to the crowd of people, all careless of the roaring, and cheered me with assurances of safety.

Nevertheless, it was in fear and trembling, and with much encouragement on his part, that I at last approached the lion's cage. Ah, I knew him on the instant. The beast! The terrible one! And on my inner vision flashed the memories of my dreams, — the midday sun shining on tall grass, the wild bull grazing quietly, the sudden parting of the grass before the swift

rush of the tawny one, his leap to the bull's
back, the crashing and the bellowing, and the
crunch crunch of bones; or again, the cool quiet
of the water-hole, the wild horse up to his knees
and drinking softly, and then the tawny one —
always the tawny one! — the leap, the screaming and the splashing of the horse, and the crunch
crunch of bones; and yet again, the sombre
twilight and the sad silence of the end of day,
and then the great full-throated roar, sudden, like
a trump of doom, and swift upon it the insane
shrieking and chattering among the trees, and
I, too, am trembling with fear and am one of the
many shrieking and chattering among the trees.

At the sight of him, helpless, within the
bars of his cage, I became enraged. I gritted
my teeth at him, danced up
and down, screaming
an incoherent
mockery and
making antic
faces. He re-
sponded, rushing
against the bars and

roaring back at me his impotent wrath. Ah, he knew me, too, and the sounds I made were the sounds of old time and intelligible to him.

My parents were frightened. "The child is ill," said my mother. "He is hysterical," said my father. I never told them, and they never knew. Already had I developed reticence concerning this quality of mine, this semi-dis-association of personality as I think I am justi-fied in calling it.

I saw the snake-charmer, and no more of the circus did I see that night. I was taken home, nervous and overwrought, sick with the inva-sion of my real life by that other life of my dreams.

I have mentioned my reticence. Only once did I confide the strangeness of it all to another. He was a boy—my chum; and we were eight years old. From my dreams I reconstructed for him pictures of that vanished world in which I do believe I once lived. I told him of the terrors of that early time, of Lop-Ear and the pranks we played, of the gibbering councils, and of the Fire People and their squatting places.

He laughed at me, and jeered, and told me tales of ghosts and of the dead that walk at night. But mostly did he laugh at my feeble fancy. I told him more, and he laughed the harder. I swore in all earnestness that these things were so, and he began to look upon me queerly. Also, he gave amazing garblings of my tales to our playmates, until all began to look upon me queerly.

It was a bitter experience, but I learned my lesson. I was different from my kind. I was abnormal with something they could not understand, and the telling of which would cause only misunderstanding. When the stories of ghosts and goblins went around, I kept quiet. I smiled grimly to myself. I thought of my nights of fear, and knew that mine were the real things — real as life itself, not attenuated vapors and surmised shadows.

For me no terrors resided in the thought of bugaboos and wicked ogres. The fall through leafy branches and the dizzy heights; the snakes that struck at me as I dodged and leaped away in chattering flight; the wild dogs that hunted

me across the open
spaces to the tim-
ber — these were
terrors concrete
and actual, hap-
penings and not im-
aginings, things of
the living flesh and
of sweat and blood.
Ogres and bugaboos
and I had been happy
bed-fellows, compared with
these terrors that made
their bed with me through-
out my childhood, and that still bed with me,
now, as I write this, full of years.

CHAPTER II

I HAVE said that in my dreams I never saw a human being. Of this fact I became aware very early, and felt poignantly the lack of my own kind. As a very little child, even, I had a feeling, in the midst of the horror of my dreaming, that if I could find but one man, only one human, I should be saved from my dreaming, that I should be surrounded no more by haunting terrors. This thought obsessed me every night of my life for years — if only I could find that one human and be saved!

I must iterate that I had this thought in the midst of my dreaming, and I take it as an evidence of the merging of my two personalities, as evidence of a point of contact between the two disassociated parts of me. My dream personality lived in the long ago, before ever man, as we know him, came to be; and my other and wake-a-day personality projected itself, to the extent of the knowledge of man's existence, into the substance of my dreams.

Perhaps the psychologists of the book will find fault with my way of using the phrase, "disassociation of personality." I know their use of it, yet am compelled to use it in my own way in default of a better phrase. I take shelter behind the inadequacy of the English language. And now to the explanation of my use, or misuse, of the phrase.

It was not till I was a young man, at college, that I got any clew to the significance of my dreams, and to the cause of them. Up to that time they had been meaningless and without apparent causation. But at college I discovered evolution and psychology, and learned the explanation of various strange mental states and experiences. For instance, there was the falling-through-space dream — the commonest dream experience, one practically known, by first-hand experience, to all men.

This, my professor told me, was a racial memory. It dated back to our remote ancestors who lived in trees. With them, being tree-dwellers, the liability of falling was an ever-present menace. Many lost their lives that way; all of them experienced terrible falls, saving themselves by clutching branches as they fell toward the ground.

Now a terrible fall, averted in such fashion, was productive of shock. Such shock was productive of molecular changes in the cerebral cells. These molecular changes were transmitted to the cerebral cells of progeny, became, in short, racial memories. Thus, when you and I, asleep or dozing off to sleep, fall through space and awake to sickening consciousness just before we strike, we are merely remembering what happened to our arboreal ancestors, and which has been stamped by cerebral changes into the heredity of the race.

There is nothing strange in this, any more than there is anything strange in an instinct. An instinct is merely a habit that is stamped into the stuff of our heredity, that is all. It will be noted, in passing, that in this falling dream which is so familiar to you and me and all of us, we never strike bottom. To strike bottom would be destruction. Those of our arboreal ancestors who struck bottom died forthwith. True, the shock of their fall was communicated to the cerebral cells, but they died immediately, before they could have progeny. You and I are descended from those that did not strike bottom; that is why you and I, in our dreams, never strike bottom.

And now we come to disassociation of personality. We never have this sense of falling when we are wide awake. Our wake-a-day personality has no experience of it. Then — and here the argument is irresistible — it must be another and distinct personality that falls when we are asleep, and that has had experience of such falling — that has, in short, a memory of past-day race experiences, just as our wake-a-day personality has a memory of our wake-a-day experiences.

It was at this stage in my reasoning that I began to see the light. And quickly the light burst upon me with dazzling brightness, illuminating and explaining all that had been weird and uncanny and unnaturally impossible in my dream experiences. In my sleep it was not my wake-a-day personality that took charge of me; it was another and distinct personality, possessing a new and totally different fund of experiences, and, to the point of my dreaming, possessing memories of those totally different experiences.

What was this personality? When had it itself lived a wake-a-day life on this planet in order to collect this fund of strange experiences? These were questions that my dreams themselves answered. He lived in the long ago, when the world was young, in that period that we call the Mid-Pleistocene. He fell from the trees but did not strike bottom. He gibbered with fear at the roaring of the lions. He was pursued by beasts of prey, struck at by deadly snakes. He chattered with his kind

in council, and he received rough usage at the hands of the Fire People in the day that he fled before them.

But, I hear you objecting, why is it that these racial memories are not ours as well, seeing that we have a vague other-personality that falls through space while we sleep?

And I may answer with another question. Why is a two-headed calf? And my own answer to this is that it is a freak. And so I answer your question. I have this other-personality and these complete racial memories because I am a freak.

But let me be more explicit. The commonest race memory

we have is the falling-through-space dream. This other-personality is very vague. About the only memory it has is that of falling. But many of us have sharper, more distinct other-personalities. Many of us have the flying dream, the pursuing-monster dream, color dreams, suffocation dreams, and the reptile and vermin dreams. In short, while this other-personality is vestigial in all of us, in some of us it is almost obliterated, while in others of us it is more pronounced. Some of us have stronger and completer race memories than others.

It is all a question of varying degree of possession of the other-personality. In myself, the degree of possession is enormous. My other-personality is almost equal in power with my own personality. And in this matter I am, as I said, a freak — a freak of heredity.

I do believe that it is the possession of this other-personality — but not so strong a one as mine — that has in some few others given rise to belief in personal reincarnation experiences. It is very plausible to such people, a most convincing hypothesis. When they have visions of scenes

they have never seen in the flesh, memories of
acts and events dating back in time, the simplest
explanation is that they have lived before.

But they make the mistake of ignoring their
own duality.   They do not recognize their other-
personality.   They think it is their own personality, that they have only one personality; and
from such a premise they can conclude only that
they have lived previous lives.

But they are wrong.   It is not reincarnation.
I have visions of myself roaming through the
forests of the Younger World; and yet it is not
myself that I see but one that is only remotely a
part of me, as my father and my grandfather
are parts of me less remote.   This other-self of
mine is an ancestor, a progenitor of my progeni-
tors in the early line of my race, himself the
progeny of a line that long before his time
developed fingers and toes and climbed up
into the trees.

I must again, at the risk of boring, repeat that
I am, in this one thing, to be considered a freak.
Not alone do I possess racial memory to an enor-
mous extent, but I possess the memories of one

particular and far-removed progenitor. And yet, while this is most unusual, there is nothing over-remarkable about it.

Follow my reasoning. An instinct is a racial memory. Very good. Then you and I and all of us receive these memories from our fathers and mothers, as they received them from their fathers and mothers. Therefore there must be a medium whereby these memories are transmitted from generation to generation. This medium is what Weismann terms the "germplasm." It carries the memories of the whole evolution of the race. These memories are dim and confused, and many of them are lost. But some strains of germplasm carry an excessive freightage of memories — are, to be scientific, more atavistic than other strains; and such a strain is mine. I am a freak of heredity, an atavistic nightmare — call me what you will; but here I am, real and alive, eating three hearty meals a day, and what are you going to do about it?

And now, before I take up my tale, I want to anticipate the doubting Thomases of psychology, who are prone to scoff, and who would otherwise surely say that the coherence of my dreams is due to overstudy and the subconscious projection of my knowledge of evolution into my dreams. In the first place, I have never been a zealous student. I graduated last of my class. I cared more for athletics, and — there is no reason I should not confess it — more for billiards.

Further, I had no knowledge of evolution until I was at college, whereas in my childhood and youth I had already lived in my dreams all the details of that other, long-ago life. I will say, however, that these details were mixed and incoherent until I came to know the science of evolution. Evolution was the key. It gave the explanation, gave sanity to the pranks of this atavistic brain of mine that, modern and normal, harked back to a past so remote as to be contemporaneous with the raw beginnings of mankind.

For in this past I know of, man, as we to-day know him, did not exist. It was in the period of his becoming that I must have lived and had my being.

CHAPTER III

THE commonest dream of my early childhood was something like this: It seemed that I was very small and that I lay curled up in a sort of nest of twigs and boughs. Sometimes I was lying on my back. In this position it seemed that I spent many hours, watching the play of sunlight on the foliage overhead and the stirring of the leaves by the wind. Often the nest itself moved back and forth when the wind was strong.

But always, while so lying in the nest, I was mastered by a feeling as of tremendous space be-

neath me. I never saw it, I never peered over
the edge of the nest to see; but I *knew* and feared
that space that lurked just beneath me and
that ever threatened me like a maw of some
all-devouring monster.

This dream, in which I was quiescent and
which was more like a condition than an experience of action, I dreamed very often in my
early childhood. But suddenly, there would
rush into the very midst of it strange forms and
ferocious happenings, the thunder and crashing
of storm, or unfamiliar landscapes such as in
my wake-a-day life I had never seen. The
result was confusion and nightmare. I could
comprehend nothing of it. There was no logic
of sequence.

You see, I did not dream consecutively.
One moment I was a wee babe of the Younger
World lying in my tree nest; the next moment
I was a grown man of the Younger World locked
in combat with the hideous Red-Eye; and the
next moment I was creeping carefully down to
the water-hole in the heat of the day. Events,
years apart in their occurrence in the Younger

World, occurred with me within the space of several minutes, or seconds.

It was all a jumble, but this jumble I shall not inflict upon you. It was not until I was a young man and had dreamed many thousand times, that everything straightened out and became clear and plain. Then it was that I got the clew of time, and was able to piece together events and actions in their proper order. Thus was I able to reconstruct the vanished Younger World as it was at the time I lived in it — or at the time my other-self lived in it. The distinction does not matter; for I, too, the modern man, have gone back and lived that early life in the company of my other-self.

For your convenience, since this is to be no sociological screed, I shall frame together the different events into a comprehensive story. For there is a certain thread of continuity and happening that runs through all the dreams. There is my friendship with Lop-Ear, for instance. Also, there is the enmity of Red-Eye, and the love of the Swift One. Taking it all in all, a fairly coherent and interesting story I am sure you will agree.

I do not remember much of my mother. Possibly the earliest recollection I have of her — and certainly the sharpest — is the following: It seemed I was lying on the ground. I was somewhat older than during the nest days, but still helpless. I rolled about in the dry leaves, playing with them and making crooning, rasping noises in my throat. The sun shone warmly and I was happy, and comfortable. I was in a little open space. Around me, on all sides, were bushes and fern-like growths, and overhead and all about were the trunks and branches of forest trees.

Suddenly I heard a sound. I sat upright and listened. I made no movement. The little noises died down in my throat, and I sat as one petrified. The sound drew closer. It was like the grunt of a pig. Then I began to hear the sounds caused by the moving of a body through the brush. Next I saw the ferns agitated by the passage of the body. Then the ferns parted, and I saw gleaming eyes, a long snout, and white tusks.

It was a wild boar. He peered at me curiously. He grunted once or twice and shifted his weight from one fore-leg to the other, at the same time moving his head from side to side  and swaying the ferns. Still I sat as one petrified, my eyes unblinking as I stared at him, fear eating at my heart.

It seemed that this movelessness and silence on my part was what was expected of me. I was not to cry out in the face of fear. It was a dictate of instinct. And so I sat there and waited for I knew not what. The boar thrust the ferns aside and stepped into the open. The curiosity went out of his eyes, and they gleamed cruelly. He tossed his head at me threateningly and advanced a step. This he did again, and yet again.

Then I screamed . . . or shrieked — I cannot describe it, but it was a shrill and terrible cry. And it seems that it, too, at this stage of the proceedings, was the thing expected of me. From not far away came an answering cry. My sounds seemed momentarily to disconcert the boar, and while he halted and shifted his weight with indecision, an apparition burst upon us.

She was like a large orang-utan, my mother, or like a chimpanzee, and yet, in sharp and definite ways, quite different. She was heavier of build than they, and had less hair. Her arms were not so long, and her legs were stouter. She wore no clothes — only her natural hair. And I can tell you she was a fury when she was excited.

And like a fury she dashed upon the scene. She was gritting her teeth, making frightful grimaces, snarling, uttering sharp and continuous cries that sounded like "kh-ah! kh-ah!" So sudden and formidable was her appearance that the boar involuntarily bunched himself together on the defensive and bristled as she swerved toward him. Then she swerved toward me. She had quite taken the breath out of him. I knew just what to do in that moment of time she had gained. I leaped to meet her, catching her about the waist and holding on hand and foot — yes, by my feet; I could hold on by them as readily as by my hands. I could feel in my tense grip the pull of the hair as her skin and her muscles moved beneath with her efforts.

As I say, I leaped to meet her, and on the instant she leaped straight up into the air, catching an overhanging branch with her hands. The next instant, with clashing tusks, the boar drove past underneath. He had recovered from his surprise and sprung forward, emitting a squeal that was almost a trumpeting. At any rate it was a call, for it was followed by the rushing of bodies through the ferns and brush from all directions.

From every side wild hogs dashed into the open space — a score of them. But my mother swung over the top of a thick limb, a dozen feet from the ground, and, still holding on to her,

"The next instant, with clashing tusks, the boar drove
past underneath."

we perched there
in safety. She was
very excited. She
chattered and
screamed, and scolded
down at the bristling,
tooth-gnashing circle
that had gath-
ered beneath. I, too,
trembling, peered down
at the angry beasts and
did my best to imitate
my mother's cries.

From the distance came
similar cries, only pitched deeper,
into a sort of roaring bass. These
grew momentarily louder, and soon
I saw him approaching, my father — at least,
by all the evidence of the times, I am driven
to conclude that he was my father.

He was not an extremely prepossessing father,
as fathers go. He seemed half man, and half
ape, and yet not ape, and not yet man. I fail
to describe him. There is nothing like him

to-day on the earth, under the earth, nor in the earth. He was a large man in his day, and he must have weighed all of a hundred and thirty pounds. His face was broad and flat, and the eyebrows over-hung the eyes. The eyes themselves were small, deep-set, and close together. He had practically no nose at all. It was squat and broad, apparently without any bridge, while the nostrils were like two holes in the face, opening outward instead of down.

The forehead slanted back from the eyes, and the hair began right at the eyes and ran up over the head. The head itself was preposterously small and was supported on an equally preposterous, thick, short neck.

There was an elemental economy about his body — as was there about all our bodies. The chest was deep, it is true, cavernously deep; but there were no full-swelling muscles, no wide-spreading shoulders, no clean-limbed straightness, no generous symmetry of outline. It represented strength, that body of my father's, strength without beauty; ferocious, primordial strength, made to clutch and gripe and rend and destroy.

His hips were thin; and the legs, lean and hairy, were crooked and stringy-muscled. In fact, my father's legs were more like arms. They were twisted and gnarly, and with scarcely the semblance of the full meaty calf such as graces your leg and mine. I remember he could not walk on the flat of his foot. This was because it was a prehensile foot, more like a hand than a foot. The great toe, instead of being in line with the other toes, opposed them, like a thumb, and its opposition to the other toes was what enabled him to get a grip with his foot. This was why he could not walk on the flat of his foot.

But his appearance was no more unusual than the manner of his coming, there to my mother and me as we perched above the angry wild pigs. He came through the trees, leaping from limb to limb and from tree to tree; and he came swiftly. I can see him now, in my wake-a-day life, as I write this, swinging along through the trees, a four-handed, hairy creature, howling

D

with rage, pausing now and again to beat his
chest with his clenched fist, leaping ten-and-
fifteen-foot gaps, catching a branch with one
hand and swinging on across another gap to
catch with his other hand and go on, never hesi-
tating, never at a loss as to how to proceed on
his arboreal way.

And as I watched him I felt in my own being,
in my very muscles themselves, the surge and
thrill of desire to go leaping from bough to
bough; and I felt also the guarantee of the
latent power in that being and in those muscles
of mine. And why not? Little boys watch
their fathers swing axes and fell trees, and feel
in themselves that some day they, too, will
swing axes and fell trees. And so with me.
The life that was in me was constituted to do
what my father did, and it whispered to me
secretly and ambitiously of aërial paths and
forest flights.

At last my father joined us. He was extremely angry. I remember the out-thrust of
his protruding underlip as he glared down at the
wild pigs. He snarled something like a dog,

and I remember that his eye-teeth were large, like fangs, and that they impressed me tremendously.

His conduct served only the more to infuriate the pigs. He broke off twigs and small branches and flung them down upon our enemies. He even hung by one hand, tantalizingly just beyond reach, and mocked them as they gnashed their tusks with impotent rage. Not content with this, he broke off a stout branch, and, holding on with one hand and foot, jabbed the infuriated beasts in the sides and whacked them across their noses.

Needless to state, my mother and I enjoyed the sport.

But one tires of all good things, and in the end, my father, chuckling maliciously the while, led the way across the trees. Now it was that my ambitions ebbed away, and I became timid, holding tightly to my mother as she climbed and swung through space. I remember when the branch broke with her weight. She had made a wide leap, and with the snap of the wood I was overwhelmed with the sickening consciousness of falling through space, the pair of us. The forest and the sunshine on the rustling leaves vanished from my eyes. I had a fading glimpse of my father abruptly arresting his progress to look, and then all was blackness.

The next moment I was awake, in my sheeted bed, sweating, trembling, nauseated. The window was up, and a cool air was blowing through the room. The night-lamp was burning calmly. And because of this I take it that the wild pigs did not get us, that we never fetched bottom; else I should not be here now, a thousand centuries after, to remember the event.

And now put yourself in my place for a moment. Walk with me a bit in my tender childhood, bed with me a night and imagine yourself dreaming such incomprehensible horrors. Remember I was an inexperienced child. I had never seen a wild boar in my life. For that matter I had never seen a domesticated pig. The nearest approach to one that I had seen was breakfast bacon sizzling in its fat. And yet here, real as life, wild boars dashed through my dreams, and I, with fantastic parents, swung through the lofty tree-spaces.

Do you wonder that I was frightened and oppressed by my nightmare-ridden nights? I was accursed. And, worst of all, I was afraid to tell. I do not know why, except that I had a feeling of guilt, though I knew no better of what I was guilty. So it was, through long years, that I suffered in silence, until I came to man's estate and learned the why and wherefore of my dreams.

CHAPTER IV

THERE is one puzzling thing about these prehistoric memories of mine. It is the vagueness of the time element. I do not always know the order of events; nor can I tell, between some events, whether one, two, or four or five years have elapsed. I can only roughly tell the passage of time by judging the changes in the appearance and pursuits of my fellows.

Also, I can apply the logic of events to the various happenings. For instance, there is no doubt whatever that my mother and I were treed by the wild pigs and fled and fell in the days before I made the acquaintance of Lop-Ear, who became what I may call my boyhood chum. And it is just as conclusive that between these two periods I must have left my mother.

I have no memory of my father than the one I have given. Never, in the years that followed, did he reappear. And from my knowledge of the times, the only explanation possible lies in that he perished shortly after the adventure with the wild pigs. That it must have been an untimely end, there is no discussion. He was in full vigor, and only sudden and violent death could have taken him off. But I know not the manner of his going — whether he was drowned in the river, or was

swallowed by a snake, or went into the stomach of old Saber-Tooth, the tiger, is beyond my knowledge.

For know that I remember only the things I saw myself, with my own eyes, in those prehistoric days. If my mother knew my father's end, she never told me. For that matter I doubt if she had a vocabulary adequate to convey such information. Perhaps, all told, the Folk in that day had a vocabulary of thirty or forty sounds.

I call them *sounds*, rather than *words*, because sounds they were primarily. They had no fixed values, to be altered by adjectives and adverbs. These latter were tools of speech not yet invented. Instead of qualifying nouns or verbs by the use of adjectives and adverbs, we qualified sounds by intonation, by changes in quantity and pitch, by retarding and by accelerating. The length of time employed in the utterance of a particular sound shaded its meaning.

We had no conjugation. One judged the tense by the context. We talked only concrete things because we thought only concrete things. Also, we depended largely on pantomime. The simplest abstraction was practically beyond our thinking; and when one did happen to think one, he was hard put to communicate it to his fellows. There were no sounds for it. He was pressing beyond the limits of his vocabulary. If he invented sounds for it, his fellows did not understand the sounds. Then it was that he fell back on pantomime, illustrating the thought wherever possible and at the same time repeating the new sound over and over again.

Thus language grew. By the few sounds we possessed we were enabled to think a short distance beyond those sounds; then came the need for new sounds wherewith to express the new thought. Sometimes, however, we thought too long a distance in advance of our sounds, managed to achieve abstractions (dim ones I grant), which we failed utterly to make known to other folk. After all, language did not grow fast in that day.

Oh, believe me, we were amazingly simple. But we did know a lot that is not known to-day. We could twitch our ears, prick them up and flatten them down at will. And we could scratch between our shoulders with ease. We could throw stones with our feet. I have done it many a time. And for that matter, I could keep my knees straight, bend forward from the hips, and touch, not the tips of my fingers, but the points of my elbows, to the ground. And as for bird-nesting — well, I only wish the twentieth-century boy could see us. But we made no collections of eggs. We ate them.

I remember — but I out-run my story.

First let me tell of Lop-Ear and our friendship. Very early in my life, I separated from my mother. Possibly this was because, after the death of my father, she took to herself a second husband. I have few recollections of him, and they are not of the best. He was a light fellow. There was no solidity to him. He was too voluble. His infernal chattering worries me even now as I think of it. His mind was too inconsequential to permit him to possess purpose. Monkeys in their cages always remind me of him. He was monkeyish. That is the best description I can give of him.

He hated me from the first. And I quickly learned to be afraid of him and his malicious pranks. Whenever he came in sight I crept close to my mother and clung to her. But I was growing older all the time, and it was inevitable that I should from time to time stray from her, and stray farther and farther. And these were the opportunities that the Chatterer waited for. (I may as well explain that we bore no names in those days; were not known by any name. For the sake of convenience I have myself given names to the various Folk I was more closely in contact with, and the "Chatterer" is the most fitting description I can find for that precious stepfather of mine. As for me, I have named myself "Big-Tooth." My eye-teeth were pronouncedly large.)

But to return to the Chatterer. He persistently terrorized me. He was always pinching me and cuffing me, and on occasion he was not above biting me. Often my mother interfered, and the way she made his fur fly was a joy to see. But the result of all this was a beautiful and unending family quarrel, in which I was the bone of contention.

No, my home-life was not happy. I smile to myself as I write the phrase. Home-life! Home! I had no home in the modern sense of the term. My home was an association, not a habitation. I lived in my mother's care, not in a house. And my mother lived anywhere, so long as when night came she was above the ground.

My mother was old-fashioned. She still clung to her trees. It is true, the more progressive members of our horde lived in the caves above the river. But my mother was suspicious and unprogressive. The trees were good enough for her. Of course, we had one particular tree in which we usually roosted, though we often roosted in other trees when nightfall caught us. In a convenient fork was a sort of rude platform of twigs and branches and creeping things. It was more like a huge bird-nest than anything else, though it was a thousand times cruder in the weaving than any bird-nest. But it had one feature that I have never seen attached to any bird-nest, namely, a roof.

Oh, not a roof such as modern man makes! Nor a roof such as is made by the lowest aborigines of to-day. It was infinitely more clumsy than the clumsiest handiwork of man — of man as we know him. It was put together in a casual, helter-skelter sort of way. Above the fork of the tree whereon we rested was a pile of dead branches and brush. Four or five adjacent forks held what I may term the various ridge-poles. These were merely stout sticks an inch or so in diameter. On them rested the

brush and branches. These seemed to have
been tossed on almost aimlessly. There was
no attempt at thatching. And I must confess
that the roof
leaked misera-
bly in a heavy
rain.

But the Chat-
terer. He made
home-life a bur-
den for both
my mother and
me — and by
home-life I mean, not the leaky nest in the tree,
but the group-life of the three of us. He was
most malicious in his persecution of me. That
was the one purpose to which he held stead-
fastly for longer than five minutes. Also, as
time went by, my mother was less eager in her
defence of me. I think, what of the continuous
rows raised by the Chatterer, that I must have
become a nuisance to her. At any rate, the
situation went from bad to worse so rapidly
that I should soon, of my own volition, have

left home. But the satisfaction of performing so independent an act was denied me. Before I was ready to go, I was thrown out. And I mean this literally.

The opportunity came to the Chatterer one day when I was alone in the nest. My mother and the Chatterer had gone away together toward the blueberry swamp. He must have planned the whole thing, for I heard him returning alone through the forest, roaring with self-induced rage as he came. Like all the men of our horde, when they were angry or were trying to make themselves angry, he stopped now and again to hammer on his chest with his fist.

I realized the helplessness of my situation, and crouched trembling in the nest. The Chatterer came directly to the tree — I remember it was an oak tree — and began to climb up. And he never ceased for a moment from his infernal row. As I have said, our language was extremely meagre, and he must have strained it by the variety of ways in which he informed me of his undying hatred of me and of his intention there and then to have it out with me.

As he climbed to the fork, I fled out the great horizontal limb. He followed me, and out I went, farther and farther. At last I was out amongst the small twigs and leaves. The Chatterer was ever a coward, and greater always than any anger he ever worked up was his caution. He was afraid to follow me out amongst the leaves and twigs. For that matter, his greater weight would have crashed him through the foliage before he could have got to me.

But it was not necessary for him to reach me, and well he knew it, the scoundrel! With a malevolent expression on his face, his beady eyes gleaming with cruel intelligence, he began teetering. Teetering! — and with me out on the very edge of the bough, clutching at the twigs that broke continually with my weight. Twenty feet beneath me was the earth.

Wildly and more wildly he teetered, grinning at me his gloating hatred. Then came the end. All four holds broke at the same time, and I fell, back-downward, looking up at him, my hands and feet still clutching the broken twigs. Luckily, there were no wild pigs under me, and my fall was broken by the tough and springy bushes.

Usually, my falls destroy my dreams, the nervous shock being sufficient to bridge the thousand centuries in an instant and hurl me wide awake into my little bed, where, perchance, I lie sweating and trembling and hear the cuckoo clock calling the hour in the hall. But this dream of my leaving home I have had many times, and never yet have I been awakened by it. Always do I crash, shrieking, down through the brush and fetch up with a bump on the ground.

Scratched and bruised and whimpering, I lay where I had fallen. Peering up through the bushes, I could see the Chatterer. He had set up a demoniacal chant of joy and was keeping time to it with his teetering. I quickly hushed my whimpering. I was no longer in the safety of the trees, and I knew the danger I ran of bringing upon myself the hunting animals by too audible an expression of my grief.

I remember, as my sobs died down, that I became interested in watching the strange light-effects produced by partially opening and closing my tear-wet eyelids. Then I began to investigate, and found that I was not so very badly damaged by my fall. I had lost some hair and hide, here and there; the sharp and jagged end of a broken branch had thrust fully an inch into my forearm; and my right hip, which had borne the brunt of my contact with the ground, was aching intolerably. But these, after all, were only petty hurts. No bones were broken, and in those days the flesh of man had finer healing qualities than it has to-day. Yet it was a severe fall, for I limped with my injured hip for fully a week afterward.

Next, as I lay in the bushes, there came upon me a feeling of desolation, a consciousness that I was homeless. I made up my mind never to return to my mother and the Chatterer. I would go far away through the terrible forest, and find some tree for myself in which to roost. As for food, I knew where to find it. For the last year at least I had not been beholden to

E

my mother for food. All she had furnished me was protection and guidance.

I crawled softly out through the bushes. Once I looked back and saw the Chatterer still chanting and teetering. It was not a pleasant sight. I knew pretty well how to be cautious, and I was exceedingly careful on this my first journey in the world.

I gave no thought as to where I was going. I had but one purpose, and that was to go away beyond the reach of the Chatterer. I climbed into the trees and wandered on amongst them for hours, passing from tree to tree and never touching the ground. But I did not go in any particular direction, nor did I travel steadily. It was my nature, as it was the nature of all my folk, to be inconsequential. Besides, I was a mere child, and I stopped a great deal to play by the way.

The events that befell me on my leaving home are very vague in my mind. My dreams do not cover them. Much has my other-self forgotten, and particularly at this very period. Nor have I been able to frame up the various

dreams so as to bridge the
gap between my leaving the home-
tree and my arrival at the caves.

I remember that several times I came to
open spaces. These I crossed in great trepi-
dation, descending to the ground and running
at the top of my speed. I remember that there
were days of rain and days of sunshine, so that
I must have wandered alone for quite a time.
I especially dream of my misery in the rain, and
of my sufferings from hunger and how I ap-
peased it. One very strong impression is of
hunting little lizards on the rocky top of an open
knoll. They ran under the rocks, and most of
them escaped; but occasionally I turned over
a stone and caught one. I was frightened away
from this knoll by snakes. They did not pursue

me. They were merely basking on flat rocks in the sun. But such was my inherited fear of them that I fled as fast as if they had been after me.

Then I gnawed bitter bark from young trees. I remember vaguely the eating of many green nuts, with soft shells and milky kernels. And I remember most distinctly suffering from a stomach-ache. It may have been caused by the green nuts, and maybe by the lizards. I do not know. But I do know that I was fortunate in not being devoured during the several hours I was knotted up on the ground with the colic.

CHAPTER V

MY vision of the scene came abruptly, as I emerged from the forest. I found myself on the edge of a large clear space. On one side of this space rose up high bluffs. On the other side was the river. The earth bank ran steeply down to the water, but here and there, in several places, where at some time slides of earth had occurred, there were run-ways. These were the drinking-places of the Folk that lived in the caves.

And this was the main abiding-place of the Folk that I had chanced upon. This was, I may say, by stretching the word, the village. My mother and the Chatterer and I, and a few other simple bodies, were what might be termed suburban residents. We were part of the horde, though we lived a distance away from it. It was only a short distance, though it had taken me, what of my wandering, all of a week to arrive.

Had I come directly, I could have covered the trip in an hour.

But to return. From the edge of the forest I saw the caves in the bluff, the open space, and the run-ways to the drinking-places. And in the open space I saw many of the Folk. I had been straying, alone and a child, for a week. During that time I had seen not one of my kind. I had lived in terror and desolation. And now, at the sight of my kind, I was overcome with gladness, and I ran wildly toward them.

Then it was that a strange thing happened. Some one of the Folk saw me and uttered a warning cry. On the instant, crying out with fear and panic, the Folk fled away. Leaping and scrambling over the rocks, they plunged into the mouths of the caves and disappeared . . . all but one, a little baby, that had been dropped in the excitement close to the base of the bluff. He was wailing dolefully. His mother dashed out; he sprang to meet her and held on tightly as she scrambled back into the cave.

I was all alone. The populous open space
had of a sudden become deserted. I sat down
forlornly and whimpered. I could not understand. Why had the Folk run away from me?
In later time, when I came to know their ways,
I was to learn. When they saw me dashing out
of the forest at top speed they concluded that
I was being pursued by some hunting animal.
By my unceremonious approach I had stampeded them.

As I sat and watched the cave-mouths I
became aware that the Folk were watching
me. Soon they were thrusting their heads out.
A little later they were calling back and forth
to one another. In the hurry and confusion it
had happened that all had not gained their
own caves. Some of the young ones had sought
refuge in other caves. The mothers did not
call for them by name, because that was an
invention we had not yet made. All were
nameless. The mothers uttered querulous, anxious cries, which were recognized by the young
ones. Thus, had my mother been there calling
to me, I should have recognized her voice

amongst the voices of a thousand mothers, and in the same way would she have recognized mine amongst a thousand.

This calling back and forth continued for some time, but they were too cautious to come out of their caves and descend to the ground. Finally one did come. He was destined to play a large part in my life, and for that matter he already played a large part in the lives of all the members of the horde. He it was whom I shall call Red-Eye in the pages of this history — so called because of his inflamed eyes, the lids being always red, and, by the peculiar effect they produced, seeming to advertise the terrible savagery of him. The color of his soul was red.

He was a monster in all ways. Physically he was a giant. He must have weighed one hundred and seventy pounds. He was the largest one of our kind I ever saw. Nor did I ever see one of the Fire People so large as he, nor one of the Tree People. Sometimes, when in the newspapers I happen upon descriptions of our modern bruisers and prizefighters, I wonder what chance the best of them would have had against him.

I am afraid not much of a chance. With one grip of his iron fingers and a pull, he could have plucked a muscle, say a biceps, by the roots, clear out of their bodies. A back-handed, loose blow of his fist could have smashed their skulls like egg-shells. With a sweep of his wicked feet (or hind-hands) he could have disembowelled them. A twist could have broken their necks, and I know that with a single crunch of his jaws he could have pierced, at the same moment, the great vein of the throat in front and the spinal marrow at the back.

He could spring twenty feet horizontally from a sitting position. He was abominably hairy. It was a matter of pride with us to be not very hairy. But he was covered with hair all over, on the inside of the arms as well as the outside, and even the ears themselves. The only places on him where the hair did not grow were the soles of his hands and feet and beneath his eyes. He was frightfully ugly, his ferocious grinning mouth and huge down-hang-

ing under-   lip being
but in har-   mony with
his terrible   eyes.

This was   Red-Eye. And
right gingerly he crept   out of his cave and
descended to the ground.   Ignoring me, he
proceeded to reconnoitre.   He bent forward
from the hips as he walked; and so far forward did he bend, and so long were his arms,
that with every step he touched the knuckles
of his hands to the ground on either side of
him.   He was awkward in the semi-erect position of walking that he assumed, and he really
touched his knuckles to the ground in order to
balance himself.   But oh, I tell you he could

run on all-fours! Now this was something at which we were particularly awkward. Furthermore, it was a rare individual among us who balanced himself with his knuckles when walking. Such an individual was an atavism, and Red-Eye was an even greater atavism. That is what he was — an atavism. We were in the process of changing our tree-life to life on the ground. For many generations we had been going through this change, and our bodies and carriage had likewise changed. But Red-Eye had reverted to the more primitive tree-dwelling type. Perforce, because he was born in our horde he stayed with us; but in actuality he was an atavism and his place was elsewhere.

Very circumspect and very alert, he moved here and there about the open space, peering through the vistas among the trees and trying to catch a glimpse of the hunting animal that all suspected had pursued me. And while he did this, taking no notice of me, the Folk crowded at the cave-mouths and watched.

At last he evidently decided that there was

no danger lurking about. He was returning from the head of the run-way, from where he had taken a peep down at the drinking-place. His course brought him near, but still he did not notice me. He proceeded casually on his way until abreast of me, and then, without warning and with incredible swiftness, he smote me a buffet on the head. I was knocked backward fully a dozen feet before I fetched up against the ground, and I remember, half-stunned, even as the blow was struck, hearing the wild uproar of clucking and shrieking laughter that arose from the caves. It was a great joke — at least in that day; and right heartily the Folk appreciated it.

Thus was I received into the horde. Red-Eye paid no further attention to me, and I was at liberty to whimper and sob to my heart's content. Several of the women gathered curiously about me, and I recognized them. I had encountered them the preceding year when my mother had taken me to the hazelnut canyons.

But they quickly left me alone, being replaced by a dozen curious and teasing young-

sters. They formed a circle around me, pointing their fingers, making faces, and poking
and pinching me. I was frightened, and for a
time I endured them, then anger got the best
of me and I sprang tooth and nail upon the
most audacious one of them — none other than
Lop-Ear himself. I have so named him because he could prick up only one of his ears.
The other ear always hung limp and without
movement. Some accident had injured the
muscles and deprived him of the use of it.

He closed with me, and we went at it for all
the world like a couple of small boys fighting.
We scratched and bit, pulled hair, clinched,
and threw each other down. I remember I
succeeded in getting on him what in my college
days I learned was called a half-Nelson. This
hold gave me the decided advantage. But I
did not enjoy it long. He twisted up one leg,
and with the foot (or hind-hand) made so
savage an onslaught upon my abdomen as to
threaten to disembowel me. I had to release
him in order to save myself, and then we went
at it again.

Lop-Ear was a year older than I, but I was several times angrier than he, and in the end he took to his heels. I chased him across the open and down a run-way to the river. But he was better acquainted with the locality and ran along the edge of the water and up another run-way. He cut diagonally across the open space and dashed into a wide-mouthed cave.

Before I knew it, I had plunged after him into the darkness. The next moment I was badly frightened. I had never been in a cave before. I began to whimper and cry out. Lop-Ear chattered mockingly at me, and, springing upon me unseen, tumbled me over. He did not risk a second encounter, however, and took himself off. I was between him and the entrance, and he did not pass me; yet he seemed to have gone away. I listened, but could get no clew as to where he was. This puzzled me, and when I regained the outside I sat down to watch.

He never came out of the entrance, of that I was certain; yet at the end of several minutes he chuckled at my elbow. Again I ran after him, and again he ran into the cave; but this time I stopped at the mouth. I dropped back a short distance and watched. He did not come out, yet, as before, he chuckled at my elbow and was chased by me a third time into the cave.

This performance was repeated several times. Then I followed him into the cave, where I searched vainly for him. I was curious. I could not understand how he eluded me. Always he went into the cave, never did he come out of it, yet always did he arrive there at my elbow and mock me. Thus did our fight transform itself into a game of hide and seek.

All afternoon, with occasional intervals, we kept it up, and a playful, friendly spirit arose

between us. In the end, he did not run away
from me, and we sat together with our arms
around each other. A little later he disclosed
the mystery of the wide-mouthed cave. Holding me by the hand he led me inside. It connected by a narrow crevice with another cave,
and it was through this that we regained the
open air.

We were now good friends. When the other
young ones gathered around to tease, he joined
with me in attacking them; and so viciously
did we behave that before long I was let alone.
Lop-Ear made me acquainted with the village.
There was little that he could tell me of conditions and customs — he had not the necessary
vocabulary; but by observing his actions I
learned much, and also he showed me places
and things.

He took me up the open space, between the
caves and the river, and into the forest beyond,
where, in a grassy place among the trees, we
made a meal of stringy-rooted carrots. After
that we had a good drink at the river and started
up the run-way to the caves.

It was in the run-way that
we came upon Red-Eye
again. The first I knew,
Lop-Ear had shrunk away
to one side and was crouching low against the bank.
Naturally and involuntarily,
I imitated him. Then it was
that I looked to see the
cause of his fear. It was
Red-Eye, swaggering down
the centre of the run-way and
scowling fiercely with his inflamed
eyes. I noticed that all the youngsters shrank away from him as we
had done, while the grown-ups regarded
him with wary eyes when he drew near, and
stepped aside to give him the centre of the path.

As twilight came on, the open space was
deserted. The Folk were seeking the safety
of the caves. Lop-Ear led the way to bed.
High up the bluff we climbed, higher than all
the other caves, to a tiny crevice that could not
be seen from the ground. Into this Lop-Ear

F

squeezed. I followed with difficulty, so narrow was the entrance, and found myself in a small rock-chamber. It was very low—not more than a couple of feet in height, and possibly three feet by four in width and length. Here, cuddled together in each other's arms, we slept out the night.

CHAPTER VI

WHILE the more courageous of the youngsters played in and out of the large-mouthed caves, I early learned that such caves were unoccupied. No one slept in them at night. Only the crevice-mouthed caves were used, the narrower the mouth the better. This was from fear of the preying animals that made life a burden to us in those days and nights.

The first morning, after my night's sleep with Lop-Ear, I learned the advantage of the narrow-mouthed caves. It was just daylight when old Saber-Tooth, the tiger, walked into the open space. Two of the Folk were already up. They made a rush for it. Whether they were panic-stricken, or whether he was too close on their heels for them to attempt to scramble up the bluff to the crevices, I do not know; but at any rate they dashed into the wide-mouthed cave wherein Lop-Ear and I had played the afternoon before.

What happened inside there was no way of telling, but it is fair to conclude that the two Folk slipped through the connecting crevice into the other cave. This crevice was too small to allow for the passage of Saber-Tooth, and he came out the way he had gone in, unsatisfied and angry. It was evident that his night's hunting had been unsuccessful and that he had expected to make a meal off of us. He caught sight of the two Folk at the other cave-mouth and sprang for them. Of course, they darted through the passageway into the first cave. He emerged angrier than ever and snarling.

Pandemonium broke loose amongst the rest of us. All up and down the great bluff, we crowded the crevices and outside ledges, and we were all chattering and shrieking in a thousand keys. And we were all making faces — snarling faces; this was an instinct with us. We were as angry as Saber-Tooth, though our anger was allied with fear. I remember that

I shrieked and made faces with the best of them. Not only did they set the example, but I felt the urge from within me to do the same things they were doing. My hair was bristling, and I was convulsed with a fierce, unreasoning rage.

For some time old Saber-Tooth continued dashing in and out of first the one cave and then the other. But the two Folk merely slipped back and forth through the connecting crevice and eluded him. In the meantime the rest of us up the bluff had proceeded to action. Every time he appeared outside we pelted him with rocks. At first we merely dropped them on him, but we soon began to whiz them down with the added force of our muscles.

This bombardment drew Saber-Tooth's attention to us and made him angrier than ever. He abandoned his pursuit of the two Folk and sprang up the bluff toward the rest of us, clawing at the crumbling rock and snarling as he clawed his upward way, At this awful sight, the last one of us sought refuge inside our caves. I know this, because I peeped out and saw the whole bluff-side deserted, save for Saber-Tooth, who had lost his footing and was sliding and falling down.

I called out the cry of encouragement, and again the bluff was covered by the screaming horde and the stones were falling faster than ever. Saber-Tooth was frantic with rage. Time and again he assaulted the bluff. Once he even gained the first crevice-entrances before he fell back, but was unable to force his way inside. With each upward rush he made, waves of fear surged over us. At first, at such times, most of us dashed inside; but some remained outside to hammer him with stones, and soon all of us remained outside and kept up the fusillade.

Never was so masterly a creature so completely baffled. It hurt his pride terribly, thus to be outwitted by the small and tender Folk. He stood on the ground and looked up at us, snarling, lashing his tail, snapping at the stones that fell near to him. Once I whizzed down a stone, and just at the right moment he looked up. It caught him full on the end of his nose,

"He sprang up the bluff, snarling as he clawed his upward way."

and he went straight up in the air, all four feet of him, roaring and caterwauling, what of the hurt and surprise.

He was beaten and he knew it. Recovering his dignity, he stalked out solemnly from under the rain of stones. He stopped in the middle of the open space and looked wistfully and hungrily back at us. He hated to forego the meal, and we were just so much meat, cornered but inaccessible. This sight of him started us to laughing. We laughed derisively and uproariously, all of us. Now animals do not like mockery. To be laughed at makes them angry. And in such fashion our laughter affected Saber-Tooth. He turned with a roar and charged the bluff again. This was what we wanted. The fight had become a game, and we took huge delight in pelting him.

But this attack did not last long. He quickly recovered his common sense, and besides, our missiles were shrewd to hurt. Vividly do I recollect the vision of one bulging eye of his, swollen almost shut by one of the stones we had thrown. And vividly do I

retain the pic-   ture of him as
he stood on   the edge
of the forest   whither he
had finally   retreated.
He was look-   ing back at
us, his writh-   ing lips lifted
clear of the very   roots of his huge
fangs, his hair bris-   tling and his tail lashing. He gave one last snarl and slid from
view among the trees.

And then such a chattering as went up.
We swarmed out of our holes, examining the
marks his claws had made on the crumbling
rock of the bluff, all of us talking at once.
One of the two Folk who had been caught in
the double cave was part-grown, half child
and half youth. They had come out proudly
from their refuge, and we surrounded them in
an admiring crowd. Then the young fellow's
mother broke through and fell upon him in a
tremendous rage, boxing his ears, pulling his
hair, and shrieking like a demon. She was a
strapping big woman, very hairy, and the
thrashing she gave him was a delight to the

horde. We roared with laughter, holding on to one another or rolling on the ground in our glee.

In spite of the reign of fear under which we lived, the Folk were always great laughers. We had the sense of humor. Our merriment was Gargantuan. It was never restrained. There was nothing half way about it. When a thing was funny we were convulsed with appreciation of it, and the simplest, crudest things were funny to us. Oh, we were great laughers, I can tell you.

The way we had treated Saber-Tooth was the way we treated all animals that invaded the village. We kept our run-ways and drinking-places to ourselves by making life miserable for the animals that trespassed or strayed upon our immediate territory. Even the fiercest hunting animals we so bedevilled that they learned to leave our places alone. We were not fighters like them; we were cunning and cowardly, and it was because of our cunning and cowardice, and our inordinate capacity for fear, that we survived in that frightfully hostile environment of the Younger World.

Lop-Ear, I figure, was a year older than I.
What his past history was he had no way of
telling me, but as I never saw anything of his
mother I believed him to be an orphan. After
all, fathers did not count in our horde. Marriage was as yet in a rude state, and couples
had a way of quarrelling and separating.
Modern man, what of his divorce institution,
does the same thing legally. But we had no
laws. Custom was all we went by, and our
custom in this particular matter was rather
promiscuous.

Nevertheless, as this narrative will show
later on, we betrayed glimmering adumbra-
tions of the monogamy that was later to give
power to, and make mighty, such tribes as
embraced it. Furthermore, even at the time
I was born, there were several faithful couples
that lived in the trees in the neighborhood of
my mother. Living in the thick of the horde
did not conduce to monogamy. It was for
this reason, undoubtedly, that the faithful
couples went away and lived by themselves.
Through many years these couples stayed to-

gether, though when the man or woman died or was eaten the survivor invariably found a new mate.

There was one thing that greatly puzzled me during the first days of my residence in the horde. There was a nameless and incommunicable fear that rested upon all. At first it appeared to be connected wholly with direction. The horde feared the northeast. It lived in perpetual apprehension of that quarter of the compass. And every individual gazed more frequently and with greater alarm in that direction than in any other.

When Lop-Ear and I went toward the northeast to eat the stringy-rooted carrots that at that season were at their best, he became unusually timid. He was content to eat the leavings, the big tough carrots and the little ropy ones, rather than to venture a short distance farther on to where the carrots were as yet untouched. When I so ventured, he scolded me and quarrelled with me. He gave me to understand that in that direction was some horrible danger, but just what the horrible danger was his paucity of language would not permit him to say.

Many a good meal I got in this fashion, while he scolded and chattered vainly at me. I could not understand. I kept very alert, but I could see no danger. I calculated always the distance between myself and the

nearest tree, and knew that to that haven of refuge I could out-foot the Tawny One, or old Saber-Tooth, did one or the other suddenly appear.

One late afternoon, in the village, a great uproar arose. The horde was animated with a single emotion, that of fear. The bluff-side swarmed with the Folk, all gazing and pointing into the northeast. I did not know what it was, but I scrambled all the way up to the safety of my own high little cave before ever I turned around to see.

And then, across the river, away into the northeast, I saw for the first time the mystery of smoke. It was the biggest animal I had ever seen. I thought it was a monster snake, up-ended, rearing its head high above the trees and swaying back and forth. And yet, somehow, I seemed to gather from the conduct of the Folk that the smoke itself was not the danger. They appeared to fear it as the token of something else. What this something else was I was unable to guess. Nor could they tell me. Yet I was soon to know, and I was to know it as a thing more terrible than the Tawny One, than old Saber-Tooth, than the snakes themselves, than which it seemed there could be no things more terrible.

CHAPTER VII

BROKEN-TOOTH was another young-
ster who lived by himself. His mother
lived in the caves, but two more children
had come after him and he had been thrust
out to shift for himself. We had witnessed the
performance during the several preceding days,
and it had given us no little glee. Broken-
Tooth did not want to go, and every time his
mother left the cave he sneaked back into it.
When she returned and found him there her
rages were delightful. Half the horde made a
practice of watching for these moments. First,
from within the cave, would come her scolding
and shrieking. Then we could hear sounds of
the thrashing and the yelling of Broken-Tooth.
About this time the two younger children joined
in. And finally, like the eruption of a minia-
ture volcano, Broken-Tooth would come flying
out.

At the end of several days his leaving home
was accomplished. He wailed his grief, unheeded, from the centre of the open space,
for at least half an hour, and then came to
live with Lop-Ear and me. Our cave
was small, but with squeez-
ing there was room for
three. I have no
recollection of
Broken-Tooth
spending more
than one night with
us, so the accident
must have happened
right away.

It came in the middle of
the day. In the morning we
had eaten our fill of the carrots,
and then, made heedless by play, we had
ventured on to the big trees just beyond. I
cannot understand how Lop-Ear got over his
habitual caution, but it must have been the
play. We were having a great time playing
tree tag. And such tag! We leaped ten or

G

fifteen-foot gaps as a matter of course. And a twenty or twenty-five foot deliberate drop clear down to the ground was nothing to us. In fact, I am almost afraid to say the great distances we dropped. As we grew older and heavier we found we had to be more cautious in dropping, but at that age our bodies were all strings and springs and we could do anything.

Broken-Tooth displayed remarkable agility in the game. He was "It" less frequently than any of us, and in the course of the game he discovered one difficult "slip" that neither Lop-Ear nor I was able to accomplish. To be truthful, we were afraid to attempt it.

When we were "It," Broken-Tooth always ran out to the end of a lofty branch in a certain tree. From the end of the branch to the ground it must have been seventy feet, and nothing intervened to break a fall. But about twenty feet lower down, and fully fifteen feet out from the perpendicular, was the thick branch of another tree.

As we ran out the limb, Broken-Tooth, facing us, would begin teetering. This naturally impeded our progress; but there was more in the teetering than that. He teetered with his back to the jump he was to make. Just as we nearly reached him he would let go. The teetering branch was like a spring-board. It threw him far out, backward, as he fell. And as he fell he turned around sidewise in the air so as to face the other branch into which he was falling. This branch bent far down under the impact, and sometimes there was an ominous crackling; but it never broke, and out of the leaves was always to be seen the face of Broken-Tooth grinning triumphantly up at us.

I was "It" the last time Broken-Tooth tried this. He had gained the end of the branch and begun his teetering, and I was creeping out after him, when suddenly there came a low warning cry from Lop-Ear. I looked down and saw him in the main fork of the tree crouching close against the trunk. Instinctively I crouched down upon the thick limb. Broken-Tooth stopped teetering, but the branch would not stop, and his body continued bobbing up and down with the rustling leaves.

I heard the crackle of a dry twig, and looking down saw my first Fire-Man. He was creeping stealthily along on the ground and peering up into the tree. At first I thought he was a wild animal, because he wore around his waist and over his shoulders a ragged piece of bearskin. And then I saw his hands and feet, and more clearly his features. He was very much like my kind, except that he was less hairy and that his feet were less like hands than ours. In fact, he and his people, as I was later to know, were far less hairy than we, though we, in turn, were equally less hairy than the Tree People.

It came to me instantly, as I looked at him. This was the terror of the northeast, of which the mystery of smoke was a token. Yet I was puzzled. Certainly he was nothing of which

"The Fire-Man peered up at him and circled around
the tree."

to be afraid. Red-Eye or any of our strong men would have been more than a match for him. He was old, too, wizened with age, and the hair on his face was gray. Also, he limped badly with one leg. There was no doubt at all that we could out-run him and out-climb him. He could never catch us, that was certain.

But he carried something in his hand that I had never seen before. It was a bow and arrow. But at that time a bow and arrow had no meaning for me. How was I to know that death lurked in that bent piece of wood? But Lop-Ear knew. He had evidently seen the Fire People before and knew something of their ways. The Fire-Man peered up at him and circled around the tree. And around the main trunk above the fork Lop-Ear circled too, keeping always the trunk between himself and the Fire-Man.

The latter abruptly reversed his circling. Lop-Ear, caught unawares, also hastily reversed, but did not win the protection of the trunk until after the Fire-Man had twanged the bow.

I saw the arrow leap up, miss Lop-Ear, glance against a limb, and fall back to the ground. I danced up and down on my lofty perch with delight. It was a game! The Fire-Man was throwing things at Lop-Ear as we sometimes threw things at one another.

The game continued a little longer, but Lop-Ear did not expose himself a second time. Then the Fire-Man gave it up. I leaned far out over my horizontal limb and chattered down at him. I wanted to play. I wanted to have him try to hit me with the thing. He saw me, but ignored me, turning his attention to Broken-Tooth, who was still teetering slightly and involuntarily on the end of the branch.

The first arrow leaped upward. Broken-Tooth yelled with fright and pain. It had reached its mark. This put a new complexion on the matter. I no longer cared to play, but crouched trembling close to my limb. A second arrow and a third soared up, missing Broken-Tooth, rustling the leaves as they passed through, arching in their flight and returning to earth.

The Fire-Man stretched his bow again. He

shifted his position, walking away several steps, then shifted it a second time. The bow-string twanged, the arrow leaped upward, and Broken-Tooth, uttering a terrible scream, fell off the branch. I saw him as he went down, turning over and over, all arms and legs it seemed, the shaft of the arrow projecting from his chest and appearing and disappearing with each revolution of his body.

Sheer down, screaming, seventy feet he fell, smashing to the earth with an audible thud and crunch, his body rebounding slightly and settling down again. Still he lived, for he moved and squirmed, clawing with his hands and feet. I remember the Fire-Man running forward with a stone and hammering him on the head . . . and then I remember no more.

Always, during my childhood, at this stage of the dream, did I wake up screaming with fright — to find, often, my mother or nurse, anxious and startled, by my bedside, passing soothing hands through my hair and telling me that they were there and that there was nothing to fear.

My next dream, in the order of succession,

begins always with the flight of Lop-Ear and myself through the forest. The Fire-Man and Broken-Tooth and the tree of the tragedy are gone. Lop-Ear and I, in a cautious panic, are fleeing through the trees. In my right leg is a burning pain; and from the flesh, protruding head and shaft from either side, is an arrow of the Fire-Man. Not only did the pull and strain of it pain me severely, but it bothered my movements and made it impossible for me to keep

up with Lop-Ear.

At last I gave up, crouching in the secure fork of a tree. Lop-Ear went right on. I called to him — most plaintively, I remember; and he stopped and looked back. Then he returned to me, climbing into the fork and examining the arrow. He tried to pull it out, but one way the flesh resisted the barbed head, and the other way it resisted the feathered shaft. Also, it hurt grievously, and I stopped him.

For some time we crouched there, Lop-Ear nervous and anxious to be gone, perpetually and apprehensively peering this way and that, and myself whimpering softly and sobbing. Lop-Ear was plainly in a funk, and yet his conduct in remaining by me, in spite of his fear, I take as a foreshadowing of the altruism and comradeship that have helped make man the mightiest of the animals.

Once again Lop-Ear tried to drag the arrow through the flesh, and I angrily stopped him. Then he bent down and began gnawing the shaft of the arrow with his teeth. As he did so he held the arrow firmly in both hands so that it would not play about in the wound, and at the same time I held on to him. I often meditate upon this scene — the two of us, half-grown cubs, in the childhood of the race, and the one mastering his fear, beating down his selfish impulse of flight, in order to stand by and succor the other. And there rises up before me all that was there foreshadowed, and I see visions of Damon and Pythias, of life-saving crews and Red Cross nurses, of martyrs and leaders of forlorn hopes, of Father Damien, and of the Christ himself, and of all the men of earth, mighty of stature, whose strength may trace back to the elemental loins of Lop-Ear and Big-Tooth and other dim denizens of the Younger World.

When Lop-Ear had chewed off the head of the arrow, the shaft was withdrawn easily enough. I started to go on, but this time it was he that stopped me. My leg was bleeding profusely. Some of the smaller veins had doubtless been ruptured. Running out to the end of a branch, Lop-Ear gathered a handful of green leaves. These he stuffed into the wound. They accomplished the purpose, for the bleeding soon stopped. Then we went on together, back to the safety of the caves.

CHAPTER VIII

WELL do I remember that first winter after I left home. I have long dreams of sitting shivering in the cold. Lop-Ear and I sit close together, with our arms and legs about each other, blue-faced and with chattering teeth. It got particularly crisp along toward morning. In those chill early hours we slept little, huddling together in numb misery and waiting for the sunrise in order to get warm.

When we went outside there was a crackle of frost under foot. One morning we discovered ice on the surface of the quiet water in the eddy where was the drinking-place, and there was a great How-do-you-do about it. Old Marrow-Bone was the oldest member of the horde, and he had never seen anything like it before. I remember the worried, plaintive look that came into his eyes as he examined the ice. (This plaintive look always came into our eyes when

we did not understand a thing, or when we felt
the prod of some vague and inexpressible desire.) Red-Eye, too, when he investigated the ice,
looked bleak and plaintive, and stared across the
river into the northeast, as though in some way
he connected the Fire People with this latest
happening.

But we found ice only on that one morning,
and that was the coldest winter we experienced.
I have no memory of other winters when it was
so cold. I have often thought that that cold
winter was a fore-runner of the countless cold
winters to come, as the ice-sheet from farther
north crept down over the face of the land. But
we never saw that ice-sheet. Many generations
must have passed away before the descendants
of the horde migrated south, or remained and
adapted themselves to the changed conditions.

Life was hit or miss and happy-go-lucky with
us. Little was ever planned, and less was executed. We ate when we were hungry, drank
when we were thirsty, avoided our carnivorous
enemies, took shelter in the caves at night, and
for the rest just sort of played along through life.

We were very curious, easily amused, and full
of tricks and pranks. There was no seriousness
about us, except when we were in danger or were
angry, in which cases the one was quickly forgotten and the other as quickly got over.

We were inconsecutive, illogical, and inconsequential. We had no steadfastness of purpose,
and it was here that the Fire People were ahead
of us. They possessed all these things of which
we possessed so little. Occasionally, however,
especially in the realm of the emotions, we were
capable of long-cherished purpose. The faith-
fulness of the monogamic couples I have referred
to may be explained as a matter of habit; but
my long desire for the Swift One cannot be so
explained, any more than can be explained the
undying enmity between me and Red-Eye.

But it was our inconsequentiality and stupidity that especially distresses me when I look
back upon that life in the long ago. Once I
found a broken gourd which happened to lie
right side up and which had been filled with
the rain. The water was sweet, and I drank it.
I even took the gourd down to the stream and

filled it with more water, some of which I drank and some of which I poured over Lop-Ear. And then I threw the gourd away. It never entered my head to fill the gourd with water and carry it into my cave. Yet often I was thirsty at night, especially after eating wild onions and watercress, and no one ever dared leave the caves at night for a drink.

Another time I found a dry gourd, inside of which the seeds rattled. I had great fun with it for a while. But it was a plaything, nothing more. And yet, it was not long after this that the using of gourds for storing water became the general practice of the horde. But I was not the inventor. The honor was due to old Marrow-Bone, and it is fair to assume that it was the necessity of his great age that brought about the innovation.

At any rate, the first member of the horde to use gourds was Marrow-Bone. He kept a supply of drinking-water in his cave, which cave belonged to his son, the Hairless One, who permitted him to occupy a corner of it. We used to see Marrow-Bone filling his gourd at the drinking-place and carrying it carefully up to his cave. Imitation was strong in the Folk, and first one, and then another and another, procured a gourd and used it in similar fashion, until it was a general practice with all of us so to store water.

Sometimes old Marrow-Bone had sick spells and was unable to leave the cave. Then it was that the Hairless One filled the gourd for him. A little later, the Hairless One deputed the task to Long-Lip, his son. And after that, even when Marrow-Bone was well again, Long-Lip continued carrying water for him. By and by, except on unusual occasions, the men never carried any water at all, leaving the task to the women and larger children. Lop-Ear and I were independent. We carried water only for ourselves, and we often mocked the young water-carriers when they were called away from play to fill the gourds.

H

Progress was slow with us. We played through life, even the adults, much in the same way that children play, and we played as none of the other animals played. What little we learned, was usually in the course of play, and was due to our curiosity and keenness of appreciation. For that matter, the one big invention of the horde, during the time I lived with it, was the use of gourds. At first we stored only water in the gourds — in imitation of old Marrow-Bone.

But one day some one of the women — I do not know which one — filled a gourd with blackberries and carried it to her cave. In no time all the women were carrying berries and nuts and roots in the gourds. The idea, once started, had to go on. Another evolution of the carrying-receptacle was due to the women. Without doubt, some woman's gourd was too small, or else she had forgotten her gourd; but be that as it may, she bent two great leaves together, pinning the seams with twigs, and carried home a bigger quantity of berries than could have been contained in the largest gourd.

So far we got, and no farther, in the transportation of supplies during the years I lived with the Folk. It never entered anybody's head to weave a basket out of willow-withes. Sometimes the men and women tied tough vines about the bundles of ferns and branches that they carried to the caves to sleep upon. Possibly in ten or twenty generations we might have worked up to the weaving of baskets. And of this, one thing is sure: if once we wove withes into baskets, the next and inevitable step would have been the weaving of cloth. Clothes would have followed, and with covering our nakedness would have come modesty.

Thus was momentum gained in the Younger World. But we were without this momentum. We were just getting started, and we could not go far in a single generation. We were without weapons, without fire, and in the raw beginnings of speech. The device of writing lay so far in the future that I am appalled when I think of it.

Even I was once on the verge of a great discovery. To show you how fortuitous was development in those days let me state that had it not been for the gluttony of Lop-Ear I might have brought about the domestication of the dog. And this was something that the Fire People who lived to the northeast had not yet achieved. They were without dogs; this I knew from observation. But let me tell you how Lop-Ear's gluttony possibly set back our social development many generations.

Well to the west of our caves was a great swamp, but to the south lay a stretch of low, rocky hills. These were little frequented for two reasons. First of all, there was no food there of the kind we ate; and next, those rocky hills were filled with the lairs of carnivorous beasts.

But Lop-Ear and I strayed over to the hills one day. We would not have strayed had we not been teasing a tiger. Please do not laugh. It was old Saber-Tooth himself. We were perfectly safe. We chanced upon him in the forest, early in the morning, and from the safety of the branches overhead we chattered down at him our dislike and hatred. And from branch to branch, and from tree to tree, we followed overhead, making an infernal row and warning all the forest-dwellers that old Saber-Tooth was coming.

We spoiled his hunting for him, anyway. And we made him good and angry. He snarled at us and lashed his tail, and sometimes he paused and stared up at us quietly for a long time, as if debating in his mind some way by which he could get hold of us. But we only laughed and pelted him with twigs and the ends of branches.

This tiger-baiting was common sport among the folk. Sometimes half the horde would follow from overhead a tiger or lion that had ventured out in the daytime. It was our revenge; for more than one member of the horde, caught unexpectedly, had gone the way of the tiger's belly or the lion's. Also, by such ordeals of helplessness and shame, we taught the hunting animals to some extent to keep out of our territory. And then it was funny. It was a great game.

And so Lop-Ear and I had chased Saber-Tooth across three miles of forest. Toward the last he put his tail between his legs and fled from our gibing like a beaten cur. We did our best to keep up with him; but when we reached the edge of the forest he was no more than a streak in the distance.

I don't know what prompted us, unless it was curiosity; but after playing around awhile, Lop-Ear and I ventured across the open ground to the edge of the rocky hills. We did not go far. Possibly at no time were we more than a hundred yards from the trees. Coming around a sharp corner of rock (we went very carefully, because we did not know what we might encounter), we came upon three puppies playing in the sun.

They did not see us, and we watched them for some time. They were wild dogs. In the rock-wall was a horizontal fissure — evidently the lair where their mother had left them, and where they should have remained had they been obedient. But the growing life, that in Lop-Ear and me had impelled us to venture away from the forest, had driven the puppies out of the cave to frolic. I know how their mother would have punished them had she caught them.

But it was Lop-Ear and I who caught them. He looked at me, and then we made a dash for it. The puppies knew no place to run except into the lair, and we headed them off. One rushed between my legs. I squatted and grabbed him. He sank his sharp little teeth into my arm, and I dropped him in the suddenness of the hurt and surprise. The next moment he had scurried inside.

Lop-Ear, struggling with the second puppy, scowled at me and intimated by a variety of sounds the

different kinds of a fool and a bungler that I
was. This made me ashamed and spurred me
to valor. I grabbed the remaining puppy by
the tail. He got his teeth into me once, and
then I got him by the nape of the neck.
Lop-Ear and I sat down, and held the puppies
up, and looked at them, and laughed.

They were snarling and yelping and crying.
Lop-Ear started suddenly. He thought he
had heard something. We looked at each
other in fear, realizing the danger of our position.
The one thing that made animals raging demons
was tampering with their young. And these
puppies that made such a racket belonged to
the wild dogs. Well we knew them, running
in packs, the terror of the grass-eating animals.
We had watched them following the herds of
cattle and bison and dragging down the calves,
the aged, and the sick. We had been chased
by them ourselves, more than once. I had seen
one of the Folk, a woman, run down by them
and caught just as she reached the shelter of
the woods. Had she not been tired out by the
run, she might have made it into a tree. She

"Well we knew them, running in packs, the terror of
the grass-eating animals."

tried, and slipped, and fell back. They made short work of her.

We did not stare at each other longer than a moment. Keeping tight hold of our prizes, we ran for the woods. Once in the security of a tall tree, we held up the puppies and laughed again. You see, we had to have our laugh out, no matter what happened.

And then began one of the hardest tasks I ever attempted. We started to carry the puppies to our cave. Instead of using our hands for climbing, most of the time they were occupied with holding our squirming captives. Once we tried to walk on the ground, but were treed by a miserable hyena, who followed along underneath. He was a wise hyena.

Lop-Ear got an idea. He remembered how we tied up bundles of leaves to carry home for beds. Breaking off some tough vines, he tied his puppy's legs together, and then, with another piece of vine passed around his neck, slung the

puppy on his back. This left him with hands and feet free to climb. He was jubilant, and did not wait for me to finish tying my puppy's legs, but started on. There was one difficulty, however. The puppy wouldn't stay slung on Lop-Ear's back. It swung around to the side and then on in front. Its teeth were not tied, and the next thing it did was to sink its teeth into Lop-Ear's soft and unprotected stomach. He let out a scream, nearly fell, and clutched a branch violently with both hands to save himself. The vine around his neck broke, and the puppy, its four legs still tied, dropped to the ground. The hyena proceeded to dine.

Lop-Ear was disgusted and angry. He abused the hyena, and then went off alone through the trees. I had no reason that I knew for wanting to carry the puppy to the cave, except that I *wanted* to; and I stayed by my task. I made the work a great deal easier by elaborating on Lop-Ear's idea. Not only did I tie the puppy's legs, but I thrust a stick through his jaws and tied them together securely.

At last I got the puppy home. I imagine
I had more pertinacity than the average Folk,
or else I should not have succeeded. They
laughed at me when they saw me lugging the
puppy up to my high little cave, but I did not
mind. Success crowned my efforts, and there
was the puppy. He was a plaything such as
none of the Folk possessed. He learned rapidly.
When I played with him and he bit me, I
boxed his ears, and then he did not try again
to bite for a long time.

I was quite taken up with him. He was
something new, and it was a characteristic of
the Folk to like new things. When I saw that
he refused fruits and vegetables, I caught
birds for him and squirrels and young rabbits.
(We Folk were meat-eaters, as well as vegetarians, and we were adept at catching small game.)
The puppy ate the meat and thrived. As well
as I can estimate, I must have had him over a
week. And then, coming back to the cave one
day with a nestful of young-hatched pheasants,
I found Lop-Ear had killed the puppy and was
just beginning to eat him. I sprang for Lop-

Ear, — the cave was small, — and we went at it tooth and nail.

And thus, in a fight, ended one of the earliest attempts to domesticate the dog. We pulled hair out in handfuls, and scratched and bit and gouged. Then we sulked and made up. After that we ate the puppy. Raw? Yes. We had not yet discovered fire. Our evolution into cooking animals lay in the tight-rolled scroll of the future.

CHAPTER IX

RED-EYE was an atavism. He was the great discordant element in our horde. He was more primitive than any of us. He did not belong with us, yet we were still so primitive ourselves that we were incapable of a coöperative effort strong enough to kill him or cast him out. Rude as was our social organization, he was, nevertheless, too rude to live in it. He tended always to destroy the horde by his unsocial acts. He was really a reversion to an earlier type, and his place was with the Tree People rather than with us who were in the process of becoming men.

He was a monster of cruelty, which is saying a great deal in that day. He beat his wives — not that he ever had more than one wife at a time, but that he was married many times. It was impossible for any woman to live with him, and yet they did live with him, out of compulsion. There was no gainsaying him.

No man was strong enough to stand against him.

Often do I have visions of the quiet hour before the twilight. From drinking-place and carrot patch and berry swamp the Folk are trooping into the open space before the caves. They dare linger no later than this, for the dreadful darkness is approaching, in which the world is given over to the carnage of the hunting animals, while the fore-runners of man hide tremblingly in their holes.

There yet remain to us a few minutes before we climb to our caves. We are tired from the play of the day, and the sounds we make are subdued. Even the cubs, still greedy for fun and antics, play with restraint. The wind from the sea has died down, and the shadows are lengthening with the last of the sun's descent. And then, suddenly, from Red-Eye's cave, breaks a wild screaming and the sound of blows. He is beating his wife.

At first an awed silence comes upon us. But as the blows and screams continue we break out into an insane gibbering of helpless rage. It is plain that the men resent Red-Eye's actions, but they are too afraid of him. The blows cease, and a low groaning dies away, while we chatter among ourselves and the sad twilight creeps upon us.

I

We, to whom most happenings were jokes, never laughed during Red-Eye's wife-beatings. We knew too well the tragedy of them. On more than one morning, at the base of the cliff, did we find the body of his latest wife. He had tossed her there, after she had died, from his cave-mouth. He never buried his dead. The task of carrying away the bodies, that else would have polluted our abiding-place, he left to the horde. We usually flung them into the river below the last drinking-place.

Not alone did Red-Eye murder his wives, but he also murdered for his wives, in order to get them. When he wanted a new wife and selected the wife of another man, he promptly killed that man. Two of these murders I saw myself. The whole horde knew, but could do nothing. We had not yet developed any government, to speak of, inside the horde. We had certain customs and visited our wrath upon the unlucky ones who violated those customs. Thus, for example, the individual who defiled a drinking-place would be attacked by every onlooker, while one who deliberately gave a false alarm was the recipient of much rough usage at our hands. But Red-Eye walked rough-shod over all our customs, and we so feared him that we were incapable of the collective action necessary to punish him.

It was during the sixth winter in our cave that Lop-Ear and I discovered that we were really growing up. From the first it had been a squeeze to get in through the entrance-crevice. This had had its advantages, however. It had prevented the larger Folk from taking our cave away from us. And it was a most desirable cave, the highest on the bluff, the safest, and in winter the smallest and warmest.

To show the stage of the mental development of the Folk, I may state that it would have been a simple thing for some of them to have driven us out and enlarged the crevice-opening. But they never thought of it. Lop-Ear and I did not think of it either until our increasing size compelled us to make an enlargement. This occurred when summer was well along and we were fat with better forage. We worked at the crevice in spells, when the fancy struck us.

At first we dug the crumbling rocks away with our fingers, until our nails got sore, when I accidentally stumbled upon the idea of using a piece of wood on the rock. This worked well. Also it worked woe. One morning early, we had scratched out of the wall quite a heap of fragments. I gave the heap a shove over the lip of the entrance. The next moment there came up from below a howl of rage. There was no need to look. We knew the voice only too well. The rubbish had descended upon Red-Eye.

We crouched down in the cave in consternation. A minute later he was at the entrance, peering in at us with his inflamed eyes and raging like a demon. But he was too large. He could not get in to us. Suddenly he went away. This was suspicious. By all we knew of Folk nature he should have remained and had out his rage. I crept to the entrance and peeped down. I could see him just beginning to mount the bluff again. In one hand he carried a long stick. Before I could divine his plan, he was back at the entrance and savagely jabbing the stick in at us.

His thrusts were prodigious. They could have disembowelled us. We shrank back against the side-walls, where we were almost out of range. But by industrious poking he got us now and again — cruel, scraping jabs with the end of the stick that raked off the hide and hair. When we screamed with the hurt, he roared his satisfaction and jabbed the harder.

I began to grow angry. I had a temper of my own in those days, and pretty considerable courage, too, albeit it was largely the courage of the cornered rat. I caught hold of the stick with my hands, but such was his strength that he jerked me into the crevice. He reached for me with his long arm, and his nails tore my flesh as I leaped back from the clutch and gained the comparative safety of the side-wall.

He began poking again, and caught me a painful blow on the shoulder. Beyond shivering with fright and yelling when he was hit, Lop-Ear did nothing. I looked for a stick with which to jab back, but found only the end of a branch, an inch through and a foot long. I threw this at Red-Eye. It did no damage, though he howled with a sudden increase of rage at my daring to strike back. He began jabbing furiously. I found a fragment of rock and threw it at him, striking him on the chest.

This emboldened me, and, besides, I was now as angry as he, and had lost all fear. I ripped a fragment of rock from the wall. The piece must have weighed two or three pounds. With all my strength I slammed it full into Red-Eye's face. It nearly finished him. He staggered backward, dropping his stick, and almost fell off the cliff.

He was a ferocious sight. His face was covered with blood, and he was snarling and gnashing his fangs like a wild boar. He wiped the blood from his eyes, caught sight of me, and roared with fury. His stick was gone, so he began ripping out chunks of crumbling rock and throwing them in at me. This supplied me with ammunition. I gave him as good as he sent, and better; for he presented a good target, while he caught only glimpses of me as I snuggled against the side-wall.

Suddenly he disappeared again. From the lip of the cave I saw him descending. All the horde had gathered outside and in awed silence was looking on. As he descended, the more timid ones scurried for their caves. I could see old Marrow-Bone tottering along as fast as he could. Red-Eye sprang out from the wall and finished the last twenty feet through the air. He landed alongside a mother who was just beginning the ascent. She screamed with fear, and the two-year-old child that was clinging to her released its grip and rolled at Red-Eye's feet. Both he and the mother reached for it, and he got it. The next moment the frail little body had whirled through the air and shattered against the wall. The mother ran to it, caught it up in her arms, and crouched over it crying.

Red-Eye started over to pick up the stick. Old Marrow-Bone had tottered into his way. Red-Eye's great hand shot out and clutched the old man by the back of the neck. I looked to see his neck broken. His body went limp as he surrendered himself to his fate. Red-Eye hesitated a moment, and Marrow-Bone, shivering terribly, bowed his head and covered his face with his crossed arms. Then Red-Eye slammed him face-downward to the ground. Old Marrow-Bone did not struggle. He lay there crying with the fear of death. I saw the Hairless One, out in the open space, beating his chest and bristling, but afraid to come forward. And then, in obedience to some whim of his erratic spirit, Red-Eye let the old man alone and passed on and recovered the stick.

He returned to the wall and began to climb up. Lop-Ear, who was shivering and peeping alongside of me, scrambled back into the cave. It was plain that Red-Eye was bent upon murder. I was desperate and angry and fairly cool. Running back and forth along the neighboring ledges, I gathered a heap of rocks at

the cave-entrance. Red-Eye was now several
yards beneath me, concealed for the moment
by an out-jut of the cliff. As he climbed, his
head came into view, and I banged a rock down.
It missed, striking the wall and shattering;
but the flying dust and grit filled his eyes and
he drew back out of view.

A chuckling and chattering arose from the
horde, that played the part of audience.
At last there was one of the Folk who dared to
face Red-Eye. As their approval and acclama-
tion arose on the air, Red-Eye snarled down at
them, and on the instant they were subdued to
silence. Encouraged by this evidence of his
power, he thrust his head into view, and by
scowling and snarling and gnashing his fangs
tried to intimidate me. He scowled horribly,
contracting the scalp strongly over the brows
and bringing the hair down from the top of the
head until each hair stood apart and pointed
straight forward.

The sight chilled me, but I mastered my
fear, and, with a stone poised in my hand,
threatened him back. He still tried to advance.

I drove the stone down at him and made a sheer miss. The next shot was a success. The stone struck him on the neck. He slipped back out of sight, but as he disappeared I could see him clutching for a grip on the wall with one hand, and with the other clutching at his throat. The stick fell clattering to the ground.

I could not see him any more, though I could hear him choking and strangling and coughing. The audience kept a death-like silence. I crouched on the lip of the entrance and waited. The strangling and coughing died down, and I could hear him now and again clearing his throat. A little later he began to climb down. He went very quietly, pausing every moment or so to stretch his neck or to feel it with his hand.

At the sight of him descending, the whole horde, with wild screams and yells, stampeded for the woods. Old Marrow-Bone, hobbling and tottering, followed behind. Red-Eye took no notice of the flight. When he reached the ground he skirted the base of the bluff and

climbed up and into his own cave. He did not look around once.

I stared at Lop-Ear, and he stared back. We understood each other. Immediately, and with great caution and quietness, we began climbing up the cliff. When we reached the top we looked back. The abiding-place was deserted, Red-Eye remained in his cave, and the horde had disappeared in the depths of the forest.

We turned and ran. We dashed across the open spaces and down the slopes unmindful of possible snakes in the grass, until we reached the woods. Up into the trees we went, and

on and on, swinging our arboreal flight until
we had put miles between us and the caves.
And then, and not till then, in the security of a
great fork, we paused, looked at each other,
and began to laugh. We held on to each other,
arms and legs, our eyes streaming tears, our
sides aching, and laughed and laughed and
laughed.

CHAPTER X

AFTER we had had out our laugh, Lop-Ear and I curved back in our flight and got breakfast in the blueberry swamp. It was the same swamp to which I had made my first journeys in the world, years before, accompanied by my mother. I had seen little of her in the intervening time. Usually, when she visited the horde at the caves, I was away in the forest. I had once or twice caught glimpses of the Chatterer in the open space, and had had the pleasure of making faces at him and angering him from the mouth of my cave. Beyond such amenities I had left my family severely alone. I was not much interested in it, and anyway I was doing very well by myself.

After eating our fill of berries, with two nestfuls of partly hatched quail-eggs for dessert, Lop-Ear and I wandered circumspectly into the woods toward the river. Here was where stood my old home-tree, out of which I had been

thrown by the Chatterer. It was still occupied.
There had been increase in the family. Clinging tight to my mother was a little baby.
Also, there was a girl, partly grown, who cautiously regarded us from one of the lower
branches. She was evidently my sister, or
half-sister, rather.

My mother recognized me, but she warned
me away when I started to climb into the
tree. Lop-Ear, who was more cautious by far
than I, beat a retreat, nor could I persuade
him to return. Later in the day, however, my
sister came down to the ground, and there and
in neighboring trees we romped and played all
afternoon. And then came trouble. She was
my sister, but that did not prevent her from
treating me abominably, for she had inherited
all the viciousness of the Chatterer. She turned
upon me suddenly, in a petty rage, and scratched
me, tore my hair, and sank her sharp little
teeth deep into my forearm. I lost my temper.
I did not injure her, but it was undoubtedly
the soundest spanking she had received up to
that time.

How she yelled and squalled. The Chatterer, who had been away all day and who was only then returning, heard the noise and rushed for the spot. My mother also rushed, but he got there first. Lop-Ear and I did not wait his coming. We were off and away, and the Chatterer gave us the chase of our lives through the trees.

After the chase was over, and Lop-Ear and I had had out our laugh, we discovered that twilight was falling. Here was night with all its terrors upon us, and to return to the caves was out of the question. Red-Eye made that impossible. We took refuge in a tree that stood apart from other trees, and high up in a fork we passed the night. It was a miserable night. For the first few hours it rained heavily, then it turned cold and a chill wind blew upon us. Soaked through, with shivering bodies and chattering teeth, we huddled in each other's arms. We missed the snug, dry cave that so quickly warmed with the heat of our bodies.

Morning found us wretched and resolved. We would not spend another such night. Re-

membering the tree-shelters of our elders, we
set to work to make one for ourselves. We built
the framework of a rough nest, and on higher
forks overhead even got in several ridge-poles
for the roof. Then the sun came out, and under
its benign influence we forgot the hardships of
the night and went off in search of breakfast.
After that, to show the inconsequentiality of
life in those days, we fell to playing. It must
have taken us all of a month, working inter-
mittently, to make our tree-house; and then,
when it was completed, we never used it again.

But I run ahead of my story. When we fell
to playing, after breakfast, on the second day
away from the caves, Lop-Ear led me a chase
through the trees and down to the river. We
came out upon it where a large slough entered
from the blueberry swamp. The mouth of
this slough was wide, while the slough itself
was practically without a current. In the dead
water, just inside its mouth, lay a tangled mass
of tree trunks. Some of these, what of the wear
and tear of freshets and of being stranded long
summers on sand-bars, were seasoned and dry

and without branches. They floated high in the water, and bobbed up and down or rolled over when we put our weight upon them.

Here and there between the trunks were water-cracks, and through them we could see schools of small fish, like minnows, darting back and forth. Lop-Ear and I became fishermen at once. Lying flat on the logs, keeping perfectly quiet, waiting till the minnows came close, we would make swift passes with our hands. Our prizes we ate on the spot, wriggling and moist. We did not notice the lack of salt.

The mouth of the slough became our favorite playground. Here we spent many hours each day, catching fish and playing on the logs, and here, one day, we learned our first lessons in navigation. The log on which Lop-Ear was lying got adrift. He was curled up on his side, asleep. A light fan of air slowly drifted the log away from the shore, and when I noticed his predicament the distance was already too great for him to leap.

At first the episode seemed merely funny to me. But when one of the vagrant impulses

K

of fear, common in that age of perpetual insecurity, moved within me, I was struck with my own loneliness. I was made suddenly aware of Lop-Ear's remoteness out there on that alien element a few feet away. I called loudly to him a warning cry. He awoke frightened, and shifted his weight rashly on the log. It turned over, sousing him under. Three times again it soused him under as he tried to climb out upon it. Then he succeeded, crouching upon it and chattering with fear.

I could do nothing. Nor could he. Swimming was something of which we knew nothing. We were already too far removed from the lower life-forms to have the instinct for swimming, and we had not yet become sufficiently man-like to undertake it as the working out of a problem. I roamed disconsolately up and down the bank, keeping as close to him in his involuntary travels as I could, while he wailed and cried till it was a wonder that he did not bring down upon us every hunting animal within a mile.

The hours passed. The sun climbed over-

head and began its descent to the west. The
light wind died down and left Lop-Ear on his
log floating around a hundred feet away. And
then, somehow, I know not how, Lop-Ear
made the great discovery. He began paddling
with his hands. At first his progress was
slow and erratic. Then he straightened out

and began laboriously
to paddle nearer and nearer. I could not
understand. I sat down and watched and
waited until he gained the shore.

But he had learned something, which was
more than I had done. Later in the afternoon, he deliberately launched out from shore
on the log. Still later he persuaded me to
join him, and I, too, learned the trick of paddling. For the next several days we could
not tear ourselves away from the slough. So
absorbed were we in our new game that we

almost neglected to eat. We even roosted in a near-by tree at night. And we forgot that Red-Eye existed.

We were always trying new logs, and we learned that the smaller the log the faster we could make it go. Also, we learned that the smaller the log the more liable it was to roll over and give us a ducking. Still another thing about small logs we learned. One day we paddled our individual logs alongside each other. And then, quite by accident, in the course of play, we discovered that when each, with one hand and foot, held on to the other's log, the logs were steadied and did not turn over. Lying side by side in this position, our outside hands and feet were left free for paddling. Our final discovery was that this arrangement enabled us to use still smaller logs and thereby gain greater speed. And there our discoveries ended. We had invented the most primitive catamaran, and we did not have sense enough to know it. It never entered our heads to lash the logs together with tough vines or stringy roots. We were content to hold the logs together with our hands and feet.

It was not until we got over our first enthusiasm for navigation and had begun to return to our tree-shelter to sleep at night, that we found the Swift One. I saw her first, gathering young acorns from the branches of a large oak near our tree. She was very timid. At first, she kept very still; but when she saw that she was discovered she dropped to the ground and dashed wildly away. We caught occasional glimpses of her from day to day, and came to look for her when we travelled back and forth between our tree and the mouth of the slough.

And then, one day, she did not run away. She waited our coming, and made soft peace-sounds. We could not get very near, however. When we seemed to approach too close, she darted suddenly away and from a safe distance uttered the soft sounds again. This continued for some days. It took a long while to get acquainted with her, but finally it was accomplished and she joined us sometimes in our play.

I liked her from the first. She was of most pleasing appearance. She was very mild. Her eyes were the mildest I had ever seen. In this she was quite unlike the rest of the girls and women of the Folk, who were born viragos. She never made harsh, angry cries, and it seemed to be her nature to flee away from trouble rather than to remain and fight.

The mildness I have mentioned seemed to emanate from her whole being. Her bodily as well as facial appearance was the cause of this. Her eyes were larger than most of her kind, and they were not so deep-set, while the lashes were longer and more regular. Nor was her nose so thick and squat. It had quite a bridge, and the nostrils opened downward. Her incisors were not large, nor was her upper lip long and down-hanging, nor her lower lip protruding. She was not very hairy, except on the outsides of arms and legs and across the shoulders; and while she was thin-hipped, her calves were not twisted and gnarly.

I have often wondered, looking back upon her from the twentieth century through the

medium of my dreams, and it has always
occurred to me that possibly she may have been
related to the Fire People. Her father, or
mother, might well have come from that higher
stock. While such things were not common,
still they did occur, and
I have seen the proof of
them with my own eyes,
even to the extent of
members of the horde
turning renegade and
going to live with the
Tree People.

All of which is neither here nor there. The
Swift One was radically different from any of
the females of the horde, and I had a liking
for her from the first. Her mildness and
gentleness attracted me. She was never rough,
and she never fought. She always ran away,
and right here may be noted the significance of
the naming of her. She was a better climber
than Lop-Ear or I. When we played tag we
could never catch her except by accident,
while she could catch us at will. She was

remarkably swift in all her movements, and she had a genius for judging distances that was equalled only by her daring. Excessively timid in all other matters, she was without fear when it came to climbing or running through the trees, and Lop-Ear and I were awkward and lumbering and cowardly in comparison.

She was an orphan. We never saw her with any one, and there was no telling how long she had lived alone in the world. She must have learned early in her helpless childhood that safety lay only in flight. She was very wise and very discreet. It became a sort of game with Lop-Ear and me to try to find where she lived. It was certain that she had a tree-shelter somewhere, and not very far away; but trail her as we would, we could never find it. She was willing enough to join with us at play in the day-time, but the secret of her abiding-place she guarded jealously.

CHAPTER XI

I T must be remembered that the description I have just given of the Swift One is not the description that would have been given by Big-Tooth, my other self of my dreams, my prehistoric ancestor. It is by the medium of my dreams that I, the modern man, look through the eyes of Big-Tooth and see.

And so it is with much that I narrate of the events of that far-off time. There is a duality about my impressions that is too confusing to inflict upon my readers. I shall merely pause here in my narrative to indicate this duality, this perplexing mixing of personality. It is I, the modern, who look back across the centuries and weigh and analyze the emotions and motives of Big-Tooth, my other self. He did not bother to weigh and analyze. He was simplicity itself. He just lived events, without ever pondering why he lived them in his particular and often erratic way.

As I, my real self, grew older, I entered more and more into the substance of my dreams. One may dream, and even in the midst of the dream be aware that he is dreaming, and if the dream be bad, comfort himself with the thought that it is only a dream. This is a common experience with all of us. And so it was that I, the modern, often entered into my dreaming, and in the consequent strange dual personality was both actor and spectator. And right often have I, the modern, been perturbed and vexed by the foolishness, illogic, obtuseness, and general all-round stupendous stupidity of myself, the primitive.

And one thing more, before I end this digression. Have you ever dreamed that you dreamed? Dogs dream, horses dream, all animals dream. In Big-Tooth's day the half-men dreamed, and when the dreams were bad they howled in their sleep. Now I, the modern, have lain down with Big-Tooth and dreamed his dreams.

This is getting almost beyond the grip of the intellect, I know; but I do know that I have done this thing. And let me tell you that the flying and crawling dreams of Big-Tooth were as vivid to him as the falling-through-space dream is to you.

For Big-Tooth also had an other-self, and when he slept that other-self dreamed back into the past, back to the winged reptiles and the clash and the onset of dragons, and beyond that to the scurrying, rodent-like life of the tiny mammals, and far remoter still, to the shore-slime of the primeval sea. I cannot, I dare not, say more. It is all too vague and complicated and awful. I can only hint of those vast and terrific vistas through which I have peered hazily at the progression of life, not upward from the ape to man, but upward from the worm.

And now to return to my tale. I, Big-Tooth, knew not the Swift One as a creature of finer facial and bodily symmetry, with long-lashed eyes and a bridge to her nose and down-opening nostrils that made toward beauty. I knew her only as the mild-eyed young female who made soft sounds and did not fight. I liked to play with her, I knew not why, to seek food in her company, and to go bird-nesting with her. And I must confess she taught me things about tree-climbing. She was very wise, very strong, and no clinging skirts impeded her movements.

It was about this time that a slight defection arose on the part of Lop-Ear. He got into the habit of wandering off in the direction of the tree where my mother lived. He had taken a liking to my vicious sister, and the Chatterer had come to tolerate him. Also, there were several other young people, progeny of the monogamic couples that lived in the neighborhood, and Lop-Ear played with these young people.

I could never get the Swift One to join with them. Whenever I visited them she dropped behind and disappeared. I remember once making a strong effort to persuade her. But

she cast backward, anxious glances, then retreated, calling to me from a tree. So it was
that I did not make a practice of accompanying
Lop-Ear when he went to visit his new friends.
The Swift One and I were good comrades, but,
try as I would, I could never find her tree-
shelter. Undoubtedly, had nothing happened,
we would have soon mated, for our liking was
mutual; but the something did happen.

One morning, the Swift One not having put
in an appearance, Lop-Ear and I were down
at the mouth of the slough playing on the
logs. We had scarcely got out on the water,
when we were startled by a roar of rage. It
was Red-Eye. He was crouching on the edge
of the timber jam and glowering his hatred at
us. We were badly frightened, for here was
no narrow-mouthed cave for refuge. But the
twenty feet of water that intervened gave us
temporary safety, and we plucked up courage.

Red-Eye stood up erect and began beating
his hairy chest with his fist. Our two logs were
side by side, and we sat on them and laughed
at him. At first our laughter was half-hearted,

tinged with fear, but as we became convinced
of his impotence we waxed uproarious. He
raged and raged at us, and ground his teeth
in helpless fury. And in our fancied security
we mocked and mocked him. We were ever
short-sighted, we Folk.

Red-Eye abruptly ceased his breast-beating
and tooth-grinding, and ran across the timber-
jam to the shore. And just as abruptly our
merriment gave way to consternation. It was
not Red-Eye's way to forego revenge so easily.
We waited in fear and trembling for whatever
was to happen. It never struck us to paddle
away. He came back with great leaps across
the jam, one huge hand filled with round,
water-washed pebbles. I am glad that he was
unable to find larger missiles, say stones weigh-
ing two or three pounds, for we were no more
than a score of feet away, and he surely would
have killed us.

As it was, we were in no small danger. Zip!
A tiny pebble whirred past with the force
almost of a bullet. Lop-Ear and I began
paddling frantically. Whiz-zip-bang! Lop-Ear

"It was Red-Eye."

screamed with sudden anguish. The pebble had struck him between the shoulders. Then I got one and yelled. The only thing that saved us was the exhausting of Red-Eye's ammunition. He dashed back to the gravel-bed for more, while Lop-Ear and I paddled away.

Gradually we drew out of range, though Red-Eye continued making trips for more ammunition and the pebbles continued to whiz about us. Out in the centre of the slough there was a slight current, and in our excitement we failed to notice that it was drifting us into the river. We paddled, and Red-Eye kept as close as he could to us by following along the shore. Then he discovered larger rocks. Such ammunition increased his range. One fragment, fully five pounds in weight, crashed on the log alongside of me, and such was its impact that it drove a score of splinters, like fiery needles, into my leg. Had it struck me it would have killed me.

And then the river current caught us. So wildly were we paddling that Red-Eye was the first to notice it, and our first warning was his yell of triumph. Where the edge of the current struck the slough-water was a series of eddies or small whirlpools. These caught our clumsy logs and whirled them end for end, back and forth and around. We quit paddling and devoted our whole energy to holding the logs together alongside each other. In the meanwhile Red-Eye continued to bombard us, the rock fragments falling about us, splashing water on us, and menacing our lives. At the same time he gloated over us, wildly and vociferously.

It happened that there was a sharp turn in the river at the point where the slough entered, and the whole main current of the river was deflected to the other bank. And toward that bank, which was the north bank, we drifted rapidly, at the same time going down-stream.

This quickly took us out of range of Red-Eye, and the last we saw of him was far out on a point of land, where he was jumping up and down and chanting a pæan of victory.

Beyond holding the two logs together, Lop-Ear and I did nothing. We were resigned to our fate, and we remained resigned until we aroused to the fact that we were drifting along the north shore not a hundred feet away. We began to paddle for it. Here the main force of the current was flung back toward the south shore, and the result of our paddling was that we crossed the current where it was swiftest and narrowest. Before we were aware, we were out of it and in a quiet eddy.

Our logs drifted slowly and at last grounded gently on the bank. Lop-Ear and I crept ashore. The logs drifted on out of the eddy and swept away down the stream. We looked at each other, but we did not laugh. We were in a strange land, and it did not enter our minds that we could return to our own land in the same manner that we had come.

We had learned how to cross a river, though

we did not know it. And this was something that no one else of the Folk had ever done. We were the first of the Folk to set foot on the north bank of the river, and, for that matter, I believe the last. That they would have done so in the time to come is undoubted; but the migration of the Fire People, and the consequent migration of the survivors of the Folk, set back our evolution for centuries.

Indeed, there is no telling how disastrous was to be the outcome of the Fire People's migration. Personally, I am prone to believe that it brought about the destruction of the Folk; that we, a branch of lower life budding toward the human, were nipped short off and perished down by the roaring surf where the river entered the sea. Of course, in such an eventuality, I remain to be accounted for; but I outrun my story, and such accounting will be made before I am done.

CHAPTER XII

I HAVE no idea how long Lop-Ear and I wandered in the land north of the river. We were like mariners wrecked on a desert isle, so far as concerned the likelihood of our getting home again. We turned our backs upon the river, and for weeks and months adventured in that wilderness where there were no Folk. It is very difficult for me to reconstruct our journeying, and impossible to do it from day to day. Most of it is hazy and indistinct, though here and there I have vivid recollections of things that happened.

Especially do I remember the hunger we endured on the mountains between Long Lake and Far Lake, and the calf we caught sleeping in the thicket. Also, there are the Tree People who dwelt in the forest between Long Lake and the mountains. It was they who chased us into the mountains and compelled us to travel on to Far Lake.

First, after we left the river, we worked toward
the west till we came to a small stream that
flowed through marshlands. Here we turned
away toward the north, skirting the marshes and
after several days arriving at what I have called
Long Lake. We spent some time around its
upper end, where we found food in plenty; and
then, one day, in the forest, we ran foul of the
Tree People. These creatures were ferocious
apes, nothing more. And yet they were not so
different from us. They were more hairy, it is

true; their legs were a trifle more twisted and
gnarly, their eyes a bit smaller, their necks a
bit thicker and shorter, and their nostrils
slightly more like orifices in a sunken surface;
but they had no hair on their faces and on the
palms of their hands and the soles of their feet,
and they made sounds similar to ours with
somewhat similar meanings. After all, the
Tree People and the Folk were not so unlike.

I found him first, a little withered, dried-up
old fellow, wrinkled-faced and bleary-eyed and
tottery. He was legitimate prey. In our world
there was no sympathy between the kinds, and
he was not our kind. He was a Tree-Man,
and he was very old. He was sitting at the
foot of a tree — evidently his tree, for we could
see the tattered nest in the branches, in which
he slept at night.

I pointed him out to Lop-Ear, and we made
a rush for him. He started to climb, but was
too slow. I caught him by the leg and dragged
him back. Then we had fun. We pinched
him, pulled his hair, tweaked his ears, and poked
twigs into him, and all the while we laughed

with streaming eyes. His futile anger was most absurd. He was a comical sight, striving to fan into flame the cold ashes of his youth, to resurrect his strength dead and gone through the oozing of the years — making woful faces in place of the ferocious ones he intended, grinding his worn teeth together, beating his meagre chest with feeble fists.

Also, he had a cough, and he gasped and hacked and spluttered prodigiously. Every time he tried to climb the tree we pulled him back, until at last he surrendered to his weakness and did no more than sit and weep. And Lop-Ear and I sat with him, our arms around each other, and laughed at his wretchedness.

From weeping he went to whining, and from whining to wailing, until at last he achieved a scream. This alarmed us, but the more we tried to make him cease, the louder he screamed. And then, from not far away in the forest, came a "Goëk! Goëk!" to our ears. To this there were answering cries, several of them, and from very far off we could hear a big, bass "Goëk! Goëk! Goëk!" Also, the "Whoo-

whoo!" call was rising in the forest all around us.

Then came the chase. It seemed it never would end. They raced us through the trees, the whole tribe of them, and nearly caught us. We were forced to take to the ground, and here we had the advantage, for they were truly the Tree People, and while they out-climbed us we out-footed them on the ground. We broke away toward the north, the tribe howling on our track. Across the open spaces we gained, and in the brush they caught up with us, and more than once it was nip and tuck. And as the chase continued, we realized that we were not their kind, either, and that the bonds between us were anything but sympathetic.

They ran us for hours. The forest seemed interminable. We kept to the glades as much as possible, but they always ended in more thick forest. Sometimes we thought we had escaped, and sat down to rest; but always, before we could recover our breath, we would hear the hateful "Whoo-whoo!" cries and the terrible "Goëk! Goëk! Goëk!" This latter sometimes terminated in a savage "Ha ha ha ha haaaaa!!!"

And in this fashion were we hunted through the forest by the exasperated Tree People. At last, by mid-afternoon, the slopes began rising higher and higher and the trees were becoming smaller. Then we came out on the grassy flanks of the mountains. Here was where we could make time, and here the Tree People gave up and returned to their forest.

The mountains were bleak and inhospitable, and three times that afternoon we tried to regain the woods. But the Tree People were lying in wait, and they drove us back. Lop-Ear and I slept that night in a dwarf tree, no larger than a bush. Here was no security, and we would have been easy prey for any hunting animal that chanced along.

In the morning, what of our new-gained respect for the Tree People, we faced into the mountains. That we had no definite plan, or even idea, I am confident. We were merely driven on by the danger we had escaped. Of our wanderings through the mountains I have

only misty memories. We were in that bleak
region many days, and we suffered much,
especially from fear, it was all so new and
strange. Also, we suffered from the cold, and
later from hunger.

It was a desolate land of rocks and foaming
streams and clattering cataracts. We climbed
and descended mighty canyons and gorges;
and ever, from every view point, there spread
out before us, in all directions, range upon

range, the unceasing
mountains. We slept
at night in holes
and crevices, and on
one cold night we
perched on top a
slender pinnacle of
rock that was almost
like a tree.

And then, at last,
one hot midday,
dizzy with hunger,
we gained the di-
vide. From this

high backbone of earth, to the north, across the diminishing, down-falling ranges, we caught a glimpse of a far lake. The sun shone upon it, and about it were open, level grass-lands, while to the eastward we saw the dark line of a wide-stretching forest.

We were two days in gaining the lake, and we were weak with hunger; but on its shore, sleeping snugly in a thicket, we found a part-grown calf. It gave us much trouble, for we knew no other way to kill than with our hands. When we had gorged our fill, we carried the remainder of the meat to the eastward forest and hid it in a tree. We never returned to that tree, for the shore of the stream that drained Far Lake was packed thick with salmon that had come up from the sea to spawn.

Westward from the lake stretched the grass-lands, and here were multitudes of bison and wild cattle. Also were there many packs of wild dogs, and as there were no trees it was not a safe place for us. We followed north along the stream for days. Then, and for what reason I do not know, we abruptly left the stream and swung to the east, and then to the southeast, through a great forest. I shall not bore you with our journey. I but indicate it to show how we finally arrived at the Fire People's country.

We came out upon the river, but we did not know it for our river. We had been lost so long that we had come to accept the condition of being lost as habitual. As I look back I see clearly how our lives and destinies are shaped by the merest chance. We did not know it was our river — there was no way of telling; and if we had never crossed it we would most probably have never returned to the horde; and I, the modern, the thousand centuries yet to be born, would never have been born.

And yet Lop-Ear and I wanted greatly to return. We had experienced homesickness on our journey, the yearning for our own kind and land; and often had I had recollections of the Swift One, the young female who made soft sounds, whom it was good to be with, and who lived by herself nobody knew where. My recollections of her were accompanied by sensations of hunger, and these I felt when I was not hungry and when I had just eaten.

But to come back to the river. Food was plentiful, principally berries and succulent roots, and on the river bank we played and lingered for days. And then the idea came to Lop-Ear. It was a visible process, the coming of the idea. I saw it. The expression in his eyes became plaintive and querulous, and he was greatly perturbed. Then his eyes went muddy, as if he had lost his grip on the inchoate thought. This was followed by the plaintive, querulous expression as the idea persisted and he clutched it anew. He looked at me, and at the river and the far shore. He tried to speak, but had no sounds with which to express the idea. The result was a gibberish that made me laugh. This angered him, and he grabbed me suddenly and threw me on my back. Of course we fought, and in the end I chased him up a tree, where he secured a long branch and poked me every time I tried to get at him.

And the idea had gone glimmering. I did not know, and he had forgotten. But the

next morning it awoke in him again. Perhaps
it was the homing instinct in him asserting
itself that made the idea persist. At any rate
it was there, and clearer than before. He led
me down to the water, where a log had grounded
in an eddy. I thought he was minded to play,
as we had played in the mouth of the slough.
Nor did I change my mind as I watched him
tow up a second log from farther down the shore.

It was not until we were on the logs, side by
side and holding them together, and had paddled
out into the current, that I learned his intention. He paused to point at the far shore,
and resumed his paddling, at the same time
uttering loud and encouraging cries. I understood, and we paddled energetically. The swift
current caught us, flung us toward the south
shore, but before we could make a landing
flung us back toward the north shore.

Here arose dissension. Seeing the north shore
so near, I began to paddle for it. Lop-Ear
tried to paddle for the south shore. The
logs swung around in circles, and we got no-
where, and all the time the forest was flashing

past as we drifted down the stream. We could not fight. We knew better than to let go the grips of hands and feet that held the logs together. But we chattered and abused each other with our tongues until the current flung us toward the south bank again. That was now the nearest goal, and together and amicably we paddled for it. We landed in an eddy, and climbed directly into the trees to reconnoitre.

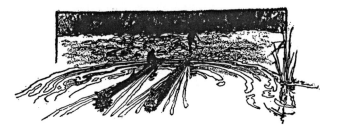

CHAPTER XIII

IT was not until the night of our first day on the south bank of the river that we discovered the Fire People. What must have been a band of wandering hunters went into camp not far from the tree in which Lop-Ear and I had elected to roost for the night. The voices of the Fire People at first alarmed us, but later, when darkness had come, we were attracted by the fire. We crept cautiously and silently from tree to tree till we got a good view of the scene.

In an open space among the trees, near to the river, the fire was burning. About it were half a dozen Fire-Men. Lop-Ear clutched me suddenly, and I could feel him tremble. I looked more closely, and saw the wizened little old hunter who had shot Broken-Tooth out of the tree years before. When he got up and walked about, throwing fresh wood upon the fire, I saw that he limped with his crippled leg. Whatever it was, it was a permanent injury. He seemed more dried up and wizened than ever, and the hair on his face was quite gray.

The other hunters were young men. I noted, lying near them on the ground, their bows and arrows, and I knew the weapons for what they were. The Fire-Men wore animal skins around their waists and across their shoulders. Their arms and legs, however, were bare, and they wore no footgear. As I have said before, they were not quite so hairy as we of the Folk. They did not have large heads, and between them and the Folk there was very little difference in the degree of the slant of the head back from the eyes.

They were less stooped than we, less springy in their movements. Their backbones and hips and knee-joints seemed more rigid. Their arms were not so long as ours either, and I did not notice that they ever balanced themselves when they walked, by touching the ground on either side with their hands. Also, their muscles

were more rounded and symmetrical than ours,
and their faces were more pleasing. Their
nose orifices opened downward; likewise the
bridges of their noses were more developed, did
not look so squat nor crushed as ours. Their
lips were less flabby and pendent, and their
eye-teeth did not look so much like fangs.
However, they were quite as thin-hipped as we,
and did not weigh much more. Take it all
in all, they were less different from us than were
we from the Tree People. Certainly, all three
kinds were related, and not so remotely related
at that.

The fire around which they sat was especially
attractive. Lop-Ear and I sat for hours, watching the flames and smoke. It was most fas-
cinating when fresh fuel was thrown on and
showers of sparks went flying upward. I
wanted to come closer and look at the fire, but
there was no way. We were crouching in the
forks of a tree on the edge of the open space,
and we did not dare run the risk of being
discovered.

The Fire-Men squatted around the fire and

slept with their heads bowed forward on their
knees. They did not sleep soundly. Their
ears twitched in their sleep, and they were
restless. Every little while one or another got
up and threw more wood upon the fire. About
the circle of light in the forest, in the darkness
beyond, roamed hunting animals. Lop-Ear
and I could tell them by their sounds. There
were wild dogs and a hyena, and for a time
there was a great yelping and snarling that
awakened on the instant the whole circle of
sleeping Fire-Men.

Once a lion and a lioness stood beneath our
tree and gazed out with bristling hair and
blinking eyes. The lion licked his chops and
was nervous with eagerness, as if he wanted
to go forward and make a meal. But the
lioness was more cautious. It was she that
discovered us, and the
pair stood

and looked up at us, silently, with twitching, scenting nostrils. Then they growled, looked once again at the fire, and turned away into the forest.

For a much longer time Lop-Ear and I remained and watched. Now and again we could hear the crashing of heavy bodies in the thickets and underbrush, and from the darkness of the other side, across the circle, we could see eyes gleaming in the firelight. In the distance we heard a lion roar, and from far off came the scream of some stricken animal, splashing and floundering in a drinking-place. Also, from the river, came a great grunting of rhinoceroses.

In the morning, after having had our sleep, we crept back to the fire. It was still smouldering, and the Fire-Men were gone. We made a circle through the forest to make sure, and then we ran to the fire. I wanted to see what it was like, and between thumb and finger I picked up a glowing coal. My cry of pain and fear, as I dropped it, stampeded Lop-Ear into the trees, and his flight frightened me after him.

The next time we came back more cautiously, and we avoided the glowing coals. We
fell to imitating the Fire-Men. We squatted
down by the fire, and with heads bent forward
on our knees, made believe to sleep. Then
we mimicked their speech, talking to each other
in their fashion and making a great gibberish.
I remembered seeing the wizened old hunter
poke the fire with a stick. I poked the fire
with a stick, turning up masses of live coals and
clouds of white ashes. This was great sport,
and soon we were coated white with the ashes.

It was inevitable that we should imitate the
Fire-Men in replenishing the fire. We tried
it first with small pieces of wood. It was a
success. The wood flamed up and crackled,
and we danced and gibbered with delight.
Then we began to throw on larger pieces of
wood. We put on more and more, until we
had a mighty fire. We dashed excitedly back
and forth, dragging dead limbs and branches
from out the forest. The flames soared higher
and higher, and the smoke-column out-towered
the trees. There was a tremendous snapping

" We, too, were Fire-Men, we thought."

and crackling and roaring. It was the most
monumental work we had ever effected with
our hands, and we were proud of it. We,
too, were Fire-Men, we thought, as we danced
there, white gnomes in the conflagration.

The dried grass and underbrush caught fire,
but we did not notice it. Suddenly a great tree
on the edge of the open space burst into flames.

We looked at
it with startled eyes. The
heat of it drove us back. An-
other tree caught, and another, and then half
a dozen. We were frightened. The monster had broken loose. We crouched down in
fear, while the fire ate around the circle and
hemmed us in. Into Lop-Ear's eyes came the
plaintive look that always accompanied incom-

prehension, and I know that in my eyes must have been the same look. We huddled, with our arms around each other, until the heat began to reach us and the odor of burning hair was in our nostrils. Then we made a dash of it, and fled away westward through the forest, looking back and laughing as we ran.

By the middle of the day we came to a neck of land, made, as we afterward discovered, by a great curve of the river that almost completed a circle. Right across the neck lay bunched several low and partly wooded hills. Over these we climbed, looking backward at the forest which had become a sea of flame that swept eastward before a rising wind. We continued to the west, following the river bank, and before we knew it we were in the midst of the abiding-place of the Fire People.

This abiding-place was a splendid strategic selection. It was a peninsula, protected on three sides by the curving river. On only one side was it accessible by land. This was the narrow neck of the peninsula, and here the several low hills were a natural obstacle.

Practically isolated from the rest of the world, the Fire People must have here lived and prospered for a long time. In fact, I think it was their prosperity that was responsible for the subsequent migration that worked such calamity upon the Folk. The Fire People must have increased in numbers until they pressed uncomfortably against the bounds of their habitat. They were expanding, and in the course of their expanding they drove the Folk before them, and settled down themselves in the caves and occupied the territory that we had occupied.

But Lop-Ear and I little dreamed of all this when we found ourselves in the Fire People's stronghold. We had but one idea, and that was to get away, though we could not forbear humoring our curiosity by peeping out upon the village. For the first time we saw the women and children of the Fire People. The latter ran for the most part naked, though the former wore skins of wild animals.

The Fire People, like ourselves, lived in caves. The open space in front of the caves sloped down to the river, and in the open space burned many small fires. But whether or not the Fire People cooked their food, I do not know. Lop-Ear and I did not see them cook. Yet it is my opinion that they surely must have performed some sort of rude cookery. Like us, they carried water in gourds from the river. There was much coming and going, and loud cries made by the women and children. The latter played about and cut up antics quite in the same way as did the children of the Folk, and they more nearly resembled the children of the Folk than did the grown Fire People resemble the grown Folk.

Lop-Ear and I did not linger long. We saw some of the part-grown boys shooting with bow and arrow, and we sneaked back into the thicker forest and made our way to the river. And there we found a catamaran, a real catamaran, one evidently made by some Fire-Man. The two logs were small and straight, and were lashed together by means of tough roots and crosspieces of wood.

This time the idea occurred simultaneously to us. We were trying to escape out of the

Fire People's territory. What better way than by crossing the river on these logs? We climbed on board and shoved off. A sudden something gripped the catamaran and flung it downstream violently against the bank. The abrupt stoppage almost whipped us off into the water. The catamaran was tied to a tree by a rope of twisted roots. This we untied before shoving off again.

By the time we had paddled well out into the current, we had drifted so far downstream that we were in full view of the Fire People's abiding-place. So occupied were we with our paddling, our eyes fixed upon the other bank, that we knew nothing until aroused by a yell from the shore. We looked around. There were the Fire People, many of them, looking at us and pointing at us, and more were crawling out of the caves. We sat up to watch, and forgot all about paddling. There was a great hullabaloo on the shore. Some of the Fire-Men discharged their bows at us, and a few of the arrows fell near us, but the range was too great.

It was a great day for Lop-Ear and me. To the east the conflagration we had started was filling half the sky with smoke. And here we were, perfectly safe in the middle of the river, encircling the Fire People's stronghold. We sat and laughed at them as we dashed by, swinging south, and southeast to east, and even to northeast, and then east again, southeast and south and on around to the west, a great double curve where the river nearly tied a knot in itself.

As we swept on to the west, the Fire People far behind, a familiar scene flashed upon our eyes. It was the great drinking-place, where we had wandered once or twice to watch the circus of the animals when they came down to drink. Beyond it, we knew, was the carrot patch, and beyond that the caves and the abiding-place of the horde. We began to paddle for the bank that slid swiftly past, and before we knew it we were down upon the drinking-places used by the horde. There were the women and children, the water carriers, a number of them, filling their gourds. At sight of us they stampeded madly up the run-ways, leaving behind them a trail of gourds they had dropped.

We landed, and of course we neglected to tie up the catamaran, which floated off down the river. Right cautiously we crept up a run-way. The Folk had all disappeared into their holes, though here and there we could see a face peering out at us. There was no sign of Red-Eye. We were home again. And that night we slept in our own little cave high up on the cliff, though first we had to evict a couple of pugnacious youngsters who had taken possession.

CHAPTER XIV

THE months came and went. The drama and tragedy of the future were yet to come upon the stage, and in the meantime we pounded nuts and lived. It was a good year, I remember, for nuts. We used to fill gourds with nuts and carry them to the pounding-places. We placed them in depressions in the rock, and, with a piece of rock in our hands, we cracked them and ate them as we cracked.

It was the fall of the year when Lop-Ear and I returned from our long adventure-journey, and the winter that followed was mild. I made frequent trips to the neighborhood of my old home-tree, and frequently I searched the whole territory that lay between the blueberry swamp and the mouth of the slough where Lop-Ear and I had learned navigation, but no clew could I get of the Swift One. She had disappeared. And I

wanted her. I was impelled by that hunger
which I have mentioned, and which was akin
to physical hunger, albeit it came often upon
me when my stomach was full. But all my
search was vain.

Life was not monotonous at the caves,
however. There was Red-Eye to be considered.
Lop-Ear and I never knew a moment's peace
except when we were in our own little cave.
In spite of the enlargement of the entrance we
had made, it was still a tight squeeze for us to
get in. And though from time to time we continued to enlarge, it was still too small for Red-
Eye's monstrous body. But he never stormed
our cave again. He had learned the lesson
well, and he carried on his neck a bulging lump
to show where I had hit him with the rock.
This lump never went away, and it was promi-
nent enough to be seen at a distance. I often
took great delight in watching that evidence of
my handiwork; and sometimes, when I was
myself assuredly safe, the sight of it caused me
to laugh.

While the other Folk would not have come

N

to our rescue had Red-Eye proceeded to tear Lop-Ear and me to pieces before their eyes, nevertheless they sympathized with us. Possibly it was not sympathy but the way they expressed their hatred for Red-Eye; at any rate they always warned us of his approach. Whether in the forest, at the drinking-places, or in the open space before the caves, they were always quick to warn us. Thus we had the advantage of many eyes in our feud with Red-Eye, the atavism.

Once he nearly got me. It was early in the morning, and the Folk were not yet up. The surprise was complete. I was cut off from the way up the cliff to my cave. Before I knew it I had dashed into the double-cave, — the cave where Lop-Ear had first eluded me long years before, and where old Saber-Tooth had come to discomfiture when he pursued the two Folk. By the time I had got through the connecting passage between the two caves, I discovered that Red-Eye was not following me. The next moment he charged into the cave from the outside. I slipped back through the passage,

and he charged out and around and in upon
me again. I merely repeated my performance
of slipping through the passage.

He kept me there half a day before he gave
up. After that, when Lop-Ear and I were
reasonably sure of gaining the double-cave, we
did not retreat up the cliff to our own cave
when Red-Eye came upon the scene. All we
did was to keep an eye on him and see that he
did not cut across our line of retreat.

It was during this winter that Red-Eye
killed his latest wife with abuse and repeated
beatings. I have called him an atavism, but
in this he was worse than an atavism, for the
males of the lower animals do not maltreat and
murder their mates. In this I take it that
Red-Eye, in spite of his tremendous atavistic
tendencies, foreshadowed the coming of man,
for it is the males of the human species only that
murder their mates.

As was to be expected, with the doing away
of one wife Red-Eye proceeded to get another.
He decided upon the Singing One. She was
the granddaughter of old Marrow-Bone, and

the daughter of the Hairless One. She was a young thing, greatly given to singing at the mouth of her cave in the twilight, and she had but recently mated with Crooked-Leg. He was a quiet individual, molesting no one and not given to bickering with his fellows. He was no fighter anyway. He was small and lean, and not so active on his legs as the rest of us.

Red-Eye never committed a more outrageous deed. It was in the quiet at the end of the day, when we began to congregate in the open space before climbing into our caves. Suddenly the Singing One dashed up a run-way from a drinking-place, pursued by Red-Eye. She ran to her husband. Poor little Crooked-Leg was terribly scared. But he was a hero. He knew that death was upon him, yet he did not run away. He stood up, and chattered, bristled, and showed his teeth.

Red-Eye roared with rage. It was an offence to him that any of the Folk should dare to withstand him. His hand shot out and clutched Crooked-Leg by the neck. The latter sank his teeth into Red-Eye's arm; but the next moment, with a broken neck, Crooked-Leg was floundering and squirming on the ground. The Singing One screeched and gibbered. Red-Eye seized her by the hair of her head and dragged her toward his cave. He handled her roughly when the climb began, and he dragged and hauled her up into the cave.

We were very angry, insanely, vociferously angry. Beating our chests, bristling, and gnashing our teeth, we gathered together in our rage. We felt the prod of gregarious instinct, the drawing together as though for united action, the impulse toward coöperation. In dim ways this need for united action was impressed upon us. But there was no way to achieve it because there was no way to express it. We did not turn to, all of us, and destroy Red-Eye, because we lacked a vocabulary. We were vaguely thinking thoughts for which there were no thought-symbols. These thought-symbols were yet to be slowly and painfully invented.

We tried to freight sound with the vague thoughts that flitted like shadows through our consciousness. The Hairless One began to chatter loudly. By his noises he expressed anger against Red-Eye and desire to hurt Red-Eye. Thus far he got, and thus far we understood. But when he tried to express the coöperative impulse that stirred within him, his noises became gibberish. Then Big-Face, with brow-bristling and chest-pounding, began to chatter. One after another of us joined in the orgy of rage, until even old Marrow-Bone was mumbling and spluttering with his cracked voice and withered lips. Some one seized a stick and began pounding a log. In a moment he had struck a rhythm. Unconsciously, our yells and exclamations yielded to this rhythm. It had a soothing effect upon us; and before we knew it, our rage forgotten, we were in the full swing of a hee-hee council.

These hee-hee councils splendidly illustrate the inconsecutiveness and inconsequentiality of the Folk. Here were we, drawn together by mutual rage and the impulse toward coöperation, led off into forgetfulness by the establishment of a rude rhythm. We were sociable and gregarious, and these singing and laughing councils satisfied us. In ways the hee-hee council was an adumbration of the councils of primitive man, and of the great national assemblies and international conventions of latter-day man. But we Folk of the Younger World lacked speech, and whenever we were so drawn together we precipitated babel, out of which arose a unanimity of rhythm that contained within itself the essentials of art yet to come. It was art nascent.

There was nothing long-continued about these rhythms that we struck. A rhythm was soon lost, and pandemonium reigned until we could find the rhythm again or start a new one. Sometimes half a dozen rhythms would be swinging simultaneously, each rhythm backed by a group that strove ardently to drown out the other rhythms.

In the intervals of pandemonium, each chattered, cut up, hooted, screeched, and danced, himself sufficient unto himself, filled with his own ideas and volitions to the exclusion of all others, a veritable centre of the

universe, divorced for the time being from any
unanimity with the other universe-centres leaping and yelling around him. Then would come
the rhythm — a clapping of hands; the beating
of a stick upon a log; the example of one that
leaped with repetitions; or the chanting of one
that uttered, explosively and regularly, with
inflection that rose and fell, "A-bang, a-bang!
A-bang, a-bang!" One after another of the
self-centred Folk would yield to it, and soon all
would be dancing or chanting in chorus. "Ha-
ah, ha-ah, ha-ah-ha!" was one of our favorite
choruses, and another was, "Eh-wah, eh-wah,
eh-wah-hah!"

And so, with mad antics, leaping, reeling,
and over-balancing, we danced and sang in the
sombre twilight of the primeval world, inducing
forgetfulness, achieving unanimity, and working ourselves up into sensuous frenzy. And
so it was that our rage against Red-Eye was
soothed away by art, and we screamed the wild
choruses of the hee-hee council until the night
warned us of its terrors, and we crept away
to our holes in the rocks, calling softly to one

another, while the stars came out
and darkness settled down.

We were afraid only of the dark.
We had no germs of religion, no
conceptions of an unseen world.
We knew only the real world, and
the things we feared were the real
things, the concrete dangers, the
flesh-and-blood animals that preyed.
It was they that made us afraid of
the dark, for darkness was the
time of the hunting animals. It
was then that they came out of
their lairs and pounced upon
one from the dark wherein
they lurked invisible.

Possibly it was out of this
fear of the real denizens of
the dark that the fear of the
unreal denizens was later to
develop and to culminate in a whole and
mighty unseen world. As imagination grew it
is likely that the fear of death increased until
the Folk that were to come projected this fear

into the dark and peopled it with spirits. I think the Fire People had already begun to be afraid of the dark in this fashion; but the reasons we Folk had for breaking up our hee-hee councils and fleeing to our holes were old Saber-Tooth, the lions and the jackals, the wild dogs and the wolves, and all the hungry, meat-eating breeds.

CHAPTER XV

LOP–EAR got married. It was the second winter after our adventure-journey, and it was most unexpected. He gave me no warning. The first I knew was one twilight when I climbed the cliff to our cave. I squeezed into the entrance and there I stopped. There was no room for me. Lop-Ear and his mate were in possession, and she was none other than my sister, the daughter of my stepfather, the Chatterer.

I tried to force my way in. There was space only for two, and that space was already occupied. Also, they had me at a disadvantage, and, what of the scratching and hair-pulling I received, I was glad to retreat. I slept that night, and for many nights, in the connecting passage of the double-cave. From my experience it seemed reasonably safe. As the two Folk had dodged old Saber-Tooth, and as I

had dodged Red-Eye, so it seemed to me that
I could dodge the hunting animals by going
back and forth between the two caves.

I had forgotten the wild dogs. They were
small enough to go through any passage that
I could squeeze through. One night they nosed
me out. Had they entered both caves at the
same time they would have got me. As it
was, followed by some of them through
the passage, I dashed out the
mouth of the other cave. Outside
were the rest of the wild dogs.
They sprang for me as I sprang
for the cliff-wall and began to
climb. One of them, a lean
and hungry brute, caught
me in mid-leap. His teeth
sank into my thigh-muscles,
and he nearly dragged me
back. He held on, but I
made no effort to dislodge him,
devoting my whole effort to climbing out of reach of the rest of the brutes.

Not until I was safe from them did I turn

my attention to that live agony on my thigh. And then, a dozen feet above the snapping pack that leaped and scrambled against the wall and fell back, I got the dog by the throat and slowly throttled him. I was a long time doing it. He clawed and ripped my hair and hide with his hind-paws, and ever he jerked and lunged with his weight to drag me from the wall.

At last his teeth opened and released my torn flesh. I carried his body up the cliff with me, and perched out the night in the entrance of my old cave, wherein were Lop-Ear and my sister. But first I had to endure a storm of abuse from the aroused horde for being the cause of the disturbance. I had my revenge. From time to time, as the noise of the pack below eased down, I dropped a rock and started it up again. Whereupon, from all around, the abuse of the exasperated Folk began afresh. In the morning I shared the dog with Lop-Ear and his wife, and for several days the three of us were neither vegetarians nor fruitarians.

Lop-Ear's marriage was not a happy one, and the consolation about it is that it did not last very long. Neither he nor I was happy during that period. I was lonely. I suffered the inconvenience of being cast out of my safe little cave, and somehow I did not make it up with any other of the young males. I suppose my long-continued chumming with Lop-Ear had become a habit.

I might have married, it is true; and most likely I should have married had it not been for the dearth of females in the horde. This dearth, it is fair to assume, was caused by the exorbitance of Red-Eye, and it illustrates the menace he was to the existence of the horde. Then there was the Swift One, whom I had not forgotten.

At any rate, during the period of Lop-Ear's marriage I knocked about from pillar to post, in danger every night that I slept, and never comfortable. One of the Folk died, and his widow was taken into the cave of another one of the Folk. I took possession of the abandoned cave, but it was wide-mouthed, and after

Red-Eye nearly trapped me in it one day, I returned to sleeping in the passage of the double-cave. During the summer, however, I used to stay away from the caves for weeks, sleeping in a tree-shelter I made near the mouth of the slough.

I have said that Lop-Ear was not happy. My sister was the daughter of the Chatterer, and she made Lop-Ear's life miserable for him. In no other cave was there so much squabbling and bickering. If Red-Eye was a Bluebeard, Lop-Ear was hen-pecked; and I imagine that Red-Eye was too shrewd ever to covet Lop-Ear's wife.

Fortunately for Lop-Ear, she died. An unusual thing happened that summer. Late, almost at the end of it, a second crop of the stringy-rooted carrots sprang up. These unexpected second-crop roots were young and juicy and tender, and for some time the carrot-patch was the favorite feeding-place of the horde. One morning, early, several score of us were there making our breakfast. On one side of me was the Hairless One. Beyond him were his father and son, old Marrow-Bone and Long-Lip. On the other side of me were my sister and Lop-Ear, she being next to me. There was no warning. On the sudden, both the Hairless One and my sister sprang and screamed. At the same instant I heard the thud of the arrows that transfixed them. The next instant they were down on the ground, floundering and gasping, and the rest of us were stampeding for the trees. An arrow drove past me and entered the ground, its feathered shaft vibrating and oscillating from the impact of its arrested flight. I remember clearly how I swerved as I ran, to go past it, and that I gave it a needlessly wide berth. I must have shied at it as a horse shies at an object it fears.

Lop-Ear took a smashing fall as he ran beside me. An arrow had driven through the calf of his leg and tripped him. He tried to run, but was tripped and thrown by it a second time. He sat up, crouching, trembling with fear, and called to me pleadingly. I dashed back. He showed me the arrow. I caught hold of it to pull it out, but the consequent hurt made him seize my hand and stop me. A flying arrow passed between us. Another struck a rock, splintered, and fell to the ground. This was too much. I pulled, suddenly, with all my might. Lop-Ear screamed as the arrow came out, and struck at me angrily. But the next moment we were in full flight again.

I looked back. Old Marrow-Bone, deserted and far behind, was tottering silently along in his handicapped race with death. Sometimes he almost fell, and once he did fall; but no more arrows were coming. He scrambled weakly to his feet. Age burdened him heavily, but he did not want to die. The three Fire-Men, who were now running forward from their forest ambush, could easily have got him, but they did not try. Perhaps he was too old and tough. But they did want the Hairless One and my sister, for as I looked back from the trees I could see the Fire-Men beating in their heads with rocks. One of the Fire-Men was the wizened old hunter who limped.

o

We went on through the trees toward the caves — an excited and disorderly mob that drove before it to their holes all the small life of the forest, and that set the blue-jays screaming impudently. Now that there was no immediate danger, Long-Lip waited for his grandfather, Marrow-Bone; and with the gap of a generation between them, the old fellow and the youth brought up our rear.

And so it was that Lop-Ear became a bachelor once more. That night I slept with him in the old cave, and our old life of chumming began again. The loss of his mate seemed to cause him no grief. At least he showed no signs of it, nor of need for her. It was the wound in his leg that seemed to bother him, and it was all of a week before he got back again to his old spryness.

Marrow-Bone was the only old member in the horde. Sometimes, on looking back upon him, when the vision of him is most clear, I note a striking resemblance between him and the father of my father's gardener. The gardener's father was very old, very wrinkled and withered; and for all the world, when he peered through his tiny, bleary eyes and mumbled with his toothless gums, he looked and acted like old Marrow-Bone. This resemblance, as a child, used to frighten me. I always ran when I saw the old man tottering along on his two canes. Old Marrow-Bone even had a bit of sparse and straggly white beard that seemed identical with the whiskers of the old man.

As I have said, Marrow-Bone was the only old member of the horde. He was an exception. The Folk never lived to old age. Middle age was fairly rare. Death by violence was the common way of death. They died as my father had died, as Broken-Tooth had died, as my sister and the Hairless One had just died — abruptly and brutally, in the full possession of their faculties, in the full swing and rush of life. Natural death? To die violently was the natural way of dying in those days.

No one died of old age among the Folk. I never knew of a case. Even Marrow-Bone did not die that way, and he was the only one in my generation who had the chance. A bad crippling, any serious accidental or temporary impairment of the faculties, meant swift death. As a rule, these deaths were not witnessed. Members of the horde simply dropped out of sight. They left the caves in the morning, and they never came back. They disappeared — into the ravenous maws of the hunting creatures.

This inroad of the Fire People on the carrot-patch was the beginning of the end, though we did not know it. The hunters of the Fire People began to appear more frequently as the time went by. They came in twos and threes, creeping silently through the forest, with their flying arrows able to annihilate distance and bring down prey from the top of the loftiest tree without themselves climbing into it. The bow and arrow was like an enormous extension of their leaping and striking muscles, so that, virtually, they could leap and kill at a hundred feet and more. This made them far more terrible than Saber-Tooth him-

self. And then they were very wise. They
had speech that enabled them more effectively
to reason, and in addition they understood
coöperation.

We Folk came to be very circumspect when
we were in the forest. We were more alert
and vigilant and timid. No longer were the
trees a protection to be relied upon. No
longer could
we perch on
a branch and
laugh down at
our carnivorous
enemies on the
ground. The
Fire People
were carnivor-
ous, with claws
and fangs a
hundred feet
long, the most
terrible of all
the hunting animals that
ranged the primeval world.

One morning, before the Folk had dispersed to the forest, there was a panic among the water-carriers and those who had gone down to the river to drink. The whole horde fled to the caves. It was our habit, at such times, to flee first and investigate afterward. We waited in the mouths of our caves and watched. After some time a Fire-Man stepped cautiously into the open space. It was the little wizened old hunter. He stood for a long time and watched us, looking our caves and the cliff-wall up and down. He descended one of the run-ways to a drinking-place, returning a few minutes later by another run-way. Again he stood and watched us carefully, for a long time. Then he turned on his heel and limped into the forest, leaving us calling querulously and plaintively to one another from the cave-mouths.

CHAPTER XVI

I FOUND her down in the old neighborhood near the blueberry swamp, where my mother lived and where Lop-Ear and I had built our first tree-shelter. It was unexpected. As I came under the tree I heard the familiar soft sound and looked up. There she was, the Swift One, sitting on a limb and swinging her legs back and forth as she looked at me.

I stood still for some time. The sight of her had made me very happy. And then an unrest and a pain began to creep in on this happiness. I started to climb the tree after her, and she retreated slowly out the limb. Just as I reached for her, she sprang through the air and landed in the branches of the next tree. From amid the rustling leaves she peeped out at me and made soft sounds. I leaped straight for her, and after an exciting chase the situation was duplicated, for there she was, making soft sounds and peeping out from the leaves of a third tree.

It was borne in upon me that somehow it was different now from the old days before Lop-Ear and I had gone on our adventure-journey. I wanted her, and I knew that I wanted her. And she knew it, too. That was why she would not let me come near her. I forgot that she was truly the Swift One, and that in the art of climbing she had been my teacher. I pursued her from tree to tree, and ever she eluded me, peeping back at me with kindly eyes, making soft sounds, and dancing and leaping and teetering before me just out of reach. The more she eluded me, the more I wanted to catch her, and the lengthening shadows of the afternoon bore witness to the futility of my effort.

As I pursued her, or sometimes rested in an adjoining tree and watched her, I noticed the change in her. She was larger, heavier, more grown-up. Her lines were rounder, her muscles fuller, and there was about her that indefinite

something of maturity that was new to her and
that incited me on. Three years she had been
gone — three years at the very least, and the
change in her was marked. I say three years;
it is as near as I can measure the time. A
fourth year may have elapsed, which I have
confused with the happenings of the other
three years. The more I think of it, the more
confident I am that it must be four years that
she was away.

Where she went, why she went, and what
happened to her during that time, I do not
know. There was no way for her to tell me,
any more than there was a way for Lop-Ear
and me to tell the Folk what we had seen when
we were away. Like us, the chance is she had
gone off on an adventure-journey, and by herself. On the other hand, it is possible that
Red-Eye may have been the cause of her going.
It is quite certain that he must have come upon
her from time to time, wandering in the woods;
and if he had pursued her there is no question
but that it would have been sufficient to
drive her away. From subsequent events, I

am led to believe that she must have travelled far to the south, across a range of mountains and down to the banks of a strange river, away from any of her kind. Many Tree People lived down there, and I think it must have been they who finally drove her back to the horde and to me. My reasons for this I shall explain later.

The shadows grew longer, and I pursued more ardently than ever, and still I could not catch her. She made believe that she was trying desperately to escape me, and all the time she managed to keep just beyond reach. I forgot everything—time, the oncoming of night, and my meat-eating enemies. I was insane with love of her, and with anger, too, because she would not let me come up with her. It was strange how this anger against her seemed to be part of my desire for her.

As I have said, I forgot everything. In racing across an open space I ran full tilt upon a colony of snakes. They did not deter me. I was mad. They struck at me, but I ducked and dodged and ran on. Then there was a python that ordinarily would have sent me screeching to a tree-top. He did run me into a tree; but the Swift One was going out of sight, and I sprang back to the ground and went on. It was a close shave. Then there was my old enemy, the hyena. From my conduct he was sure something was going to happen, and he followed me for an hour. Once we exasperated a band of wild pigs, and they took after us. The Swift One dared a wide leap between trees that was too much for me. I had to take to the ground. There were the pigs. I didn't care. I struck the earth within a yard of the nearest one. They flanked me as I ran, and chased me into two different trees out of the line of my pursuit of the Swift One. I ventured the ground again, doubled back, and crossed a wide open space, with the whole band grunting, bristling, and tusk-gnashing at my heels.

If I had tripped or stumbled in that open space, there would have been no chance for me. But I didn't. And I didn't care whether I did or not. I was in such mood that I would have faced old Saber-Tooth himself, or a score of arrow-shooting Fire People. Such was the madness of love . . . with me. With the Swift One it was different. She was very wise. She did not take any real risks, and I remember, on looking back across the centuries to that wild love-chase, that when the pigs delayed me she did not run away very fast, but waited, rather, for me to take up the pursuit again. Also, she directed her retreat before me, going always in the direction she wanted to go.

At last came the dark. She led me around the mossy shoulder of a canyon wall that outjutted among the trees. After that we penetrated a dense mass of underbrush that scraped and ripped me in passing. But she never ruffled a hair. She knew the way. In the midst of the thicket was a large oak. I was very close to her when she climbed it; and in the forks, in the nest-shelter I had sought so long and vainly, I caught her.

The hyena had taken our trail again, and he now sat down on the ground and made hungry noises. But we did not mind, and we laughed at him when he snarled and went away through the thicket. It was the spring-time, and the night noises were many and varied. As was the custom at that time of the year, there was much fighting among the animals. From the nest we could hear the squealing and neighing of wild horses, the trumpeting of elephants, and the roaring of lions. But the moon came out, and the air was warm, and we laughed and were unafraid.

I remember, next morning, that we came upon two ruffled cock-birds that fought so ardently that I went right up to them and caught them by their necks. Thus did the Swift One and I get our wedding breakfast. They were deli- cious. It was easy to catch birds in the spring of the

year. There was one night that year when two elk fought in the moonlight, while the Swift One and I watched from the trees; and we saw a lion and lioness crawl up to them unheeded, and kill them as they fought.

There is no telling how long we might have lived in the Swift One's tree-shelter. But one day, while we were away, the tree was struck by lightning. Great limbs were riven, and the nest was demolished. I started to rebuild, but the Swift One would have nothing to do with it. As I was to learn, she was greatly afraid of lightning, and I could not persuade her back into the tree. So it came about, our honeymoon over, that we went to the caves to

live. As Lop-Ear had evicted me from the
cave when he got married, I now evicted him;
and the Swift One and I settled down in it,
while he slept at night in the connecting passage
of the double cave.

And with our coming to live with the horde
came trouble. Red-Eye had had I don't know
how many wives since the Singing One. She
had gone the way of the rest. At present he
had a little, soft, spiritless thing that whimpered and wept all the time, whether he beat her
or not; and her passing was a question of very
little time. Before she passed, even, Red-Eye
set his eyes on the Swift One; and when she
passed, the persecution of the Swift One
began.

Well for her that she was the Swift One, that
she had that amazing aptitude for swift flight
through the trees. She needed all her wisdom
and daring in order to keep out of the clutches
of Red-Eye. I could not help her. He was
so powerful a monster that he could have torn
me limb from limb. As it was, to my death I
carried an injured shoulder that ached and went

lame in rainy weather and that was a mark of his handiwork.

The Swift One was sick at the time I received this injury. It must have been a touch of the malaria from which we sometimes suffered; but whatever it was, it made her dull and heavy. She did not have the accustomed spring to her muscles, and was indeed in poor shape for flight when Red-Eye cornered her near the lair of the wild dogs, several miles south from the caves. Usually, she would have circled around him, beaten him in the straightaway, and gained the protection of our small-mouthed cave. But she could not circle him. She was too dull and slow. Each time he headed her off, until she gave over the attempt and devoted her energies wholly to keeping out of his clutches.

Had she not been sick it would have been child's play for her to elude him; but as it was, it required all her caution and cunning. It was to her advantage that she could travel on thinner branches than he, and make wider leaps. Also, she was an unerring judge of distance, and she

had an instinct for knowing the strength of
twigs, branches, and rotten limbs.

It was an interminable chase. Round and
round and back and forth for long stretches
through the forest they dashed. There was
great excitement among the other Folk. They
set up a wild chattering, that was loudest when
Red-Eye was at a distance, and that hushed
when the chase led him near. They were
impotent onlookers. The females screeched
and gibbered, and the males beat their chests
in helpless rage. Big Face was especially
angry, and though he hushed his racket
when Red-Eye drew near, he did not hush
it to the extent the others did.

As for me, I played no brave part. I know
I was anything but a hero. Besides, of what
use would it have been for me to encounter
Red-Eye? He was the mighty monster, the
abysmal brute, and there was no hope for
me in a conflict of strength. He would have
killed me, and the situation would have remained unchanged. He would have caught
the Swift One before she could have gained the

P

cave. As it was, I could only look on in helpless fury, and dodge out of the way and cease
my raging when he came too near.

The hours passed. It was late afternoon.
And still the chase went on. Red-Eye was
bent upon exhausting the Swift One. He
deliberately ran her down. After a long time
she began to tire and could no longer maintain
her headlong flight. Then it was that she
began going far out on the thinnest branches,
where he could not follow. Thus she might
have got a breathing spell, but Red-Eye was
fiendish. Unable to follow her, he dislodged
her by shaking her off. With all his strength
and weight, he would shake the branch back
and forth until he snapped her off as one would
snap a fly from a whip-lash. The first time,
she saved herself by falling into branches
lower down. Another time, though they did
not save her from the ground, they broke her
fall. Still another time, so fiercely did he snap
her from the branch, she was flung clear across
a gap into another tree. It was remarkable,
the way she gripped and saved herself. Only

when driven to it did she seek the temporary
safety of the thin branches. But she was so
tired that she could not otherwise avoid him,
and time after time she was compelled to take
to the thin branches.
Still the chase
went on, and still
the Folk screeched,
beat their
chests,
and gnashed their teeth. Then
came the end. It was almost
twilight. Trembling, panting,
struggling for breath, the Swift
One clung pitiably to a high thin
branch. It was thirty feet to the
ground, and nothing intervened. Red-
Eye swung back and forth on the
branch farther down. It became a pendulum,
swinging wider and wider with every lunge of
his weight. Then he reversed suddenly, just
before the downward swing was completed.
Her grips were torn loose, and, screaming,
she was hurled toward the ground.

But she righted herself in mid-air and descended feet first. Ordinarily, from such a height, the spring in her legs would have eased the shock of impact with the ground. But she was exhausted. She could not exercise this spring. Her legs gave under her, having only partly met the shock, and she crashed on over on her side. This, as it turned out, did not injure her, but it did knock the breath from her lungs. She lay helpless and struggling for air.

Red-Eye rushed upon her and seized her. With his gnarly fingers twisted into the hair of her head, he stood up and roared in triumph and defiance at the awed Folk that watched from the trees. Then it was that I went mad. Caution was thrown to the winds; forgotten was the will to live of my flesh. Even as Red-Eye roared, from behind I dashed upon him. So unexpected was my charge that I knocked him off his feet. I twined my arms and legs around him and strove to hold him down. This would have been impossible to accomplish had he not held tightly with one hand to the Swift One's hair.

Encouraged by my conduct, Big-Face became a sudden ally. He charged in, sank his teeth in Red-Eye's arm, and ripped and tore at his face. This was the time for the rest of the Folk to have joined in. It was the chance to do for Red-Eye for all time. But they remained afraid in the trees.

It was inevitable that Red-Eye should win in the struggle against the two of us. The reason he did not finish us off immediately was that the Swift One clogged his movements. She had regained her breath and was beginning to resist. He would not release his clutch on her hair, and this handicapped him. He got a grip on my arm. It was the beginning of the end for me. He began to draw me toward him into a position where he could sink his teeth into my throat. His mouth was open, and he was grinning. And yet, though he had just begun to exert his strength, in that moment he wrenched my shoulder so that I suffered from it for the remainder of my life.

And in that moment something happened. There was no warning. A great body smashed down upon the four of us locked together. We were driven violently apart and rolled over and over, and in the suddenness of surprise we released our holds on one another. At the moment of the shock, Big-Face screamed terribly. I did not know what had happened, though I smelled tiger and caught a glimpse of striped fur as I sprang for a tree.

It was old Saber-Tooth. Aroused in his lair by the noise we had made, he had crept upon us unnoticed. The Swift One gained the next tree to mine, and I immediately joined her. I put my arms around her and held her close to me while she whimpered and cried softly. From the ground came a snarling, and crunching of bones. It was Saber-Tooth making his supper off of what had been Big-Face. From beyond, with inflamed rims and eyes, Red-Eye peered down. Here was a monster mightier than he. The Swift One and I turned and went away quietly through the trees toward the cave, while the Folk gathered overhead and showered down abuse and twigs and branches upon their ancient enemy. He lashed his tail and snarled, but went on eating.

And in such fashion were we saved. It was a mere accident — the sheerest accident. Else would I have died, there in Red-Eye's clutch, and there would have been no bridging of time to the tune of a thousand centuries down to a progeny that reads newspapers and rides on electric cars — ay, and that writes narratives of bygone happenings even as this is written.

CHAPTER XVII

IT was in the early fall of the following year that it happened. After his failure to get the Swift One, Red-Eye had taken another wife; and, strange to relate, she was still alive. Stranger still, they had a baby several months old — Red-Eye's first child. His previous wives had never lived long enough to bear him children. The year had gone well for all of us. The weather had been exceptionally mild and food plentiful. I remember especially the turnips of that year. The nut crop was also very heavy, and the wild plums were larger and sweeter than usual.

In short, it was a golden year. And then it happened. It was in the early morning, and we were surprised in our caves. In the chill gray light we awoke from sleep, most of us, to encounter death. The Swift One and I were aroused by a pandemonium of screeching and gibbering. Our cave was the highest of all on the cliff, and we crept to the mouth and peered down. The open space was filled with the Fire People. Their cries and yells were added to the clamor, but they had order and plan, while we Folk had none. Each one of us fought and acted for himself, and no one of us knew the extent of the calamity that was befalling us.

By the time we got to stone-throwing, the Fire People had massed thick at the base of the cliff. Our first volley must have mashed some heads, for when they swerved back from the cliff three of their number were left upon the ground. These were struggling and floundering, and one was trying to crawl away. But we fixed them. By this time we males were roaring with rage, and we rained rocks upon the three men that were down. Several of the Fire-Men returned to drag them into safety, but our rocks drove the rescuers back. The Fire People became enraged. Also, they became cautious. In spite of their angry yells, they kept at a distance and sent flights of arrows against us. This put an end to the rock-throwing. By the time half a dozen of us had been killed and a score injured, the rest of us retreated inside our caves. I was not out of range in my lofty cave, but the distance was great enough to spoil effective shooting, and the Fire People did not waste many arrows on me. Furthermore, I was curious. I wanted to see. While the Swift One remained well inside the cave, trembling with fear and making low wailing sounds because I would not come in, I crouched at the entrance and watched.

The fighting had now become intermittent. It was a sort of deadlock. We were in the caves, and the question with the Fire People was how to get us out. They did not dare come in after us, and in general we would not expose ourselves to their arrows. Occasionally, when one of them drew in close to the base of the cliff, one or another of the Folk would smash a rock down. In return, he would be transfixed by half a dozen arrows. This ruse worked well for some time, but finally the Folk no longer were inveigled into showing themselves. The deadlock was complete.

Behind the Fire People I could see the little wizened old hunter directing it all. They obeyed him, and went here and there at his commands. Some of them went into the forest and returned with loads of dry wood, leaves, and grass. All the Fire People drew in closer. While most of them stood by with bows and arrows, ready to shoot any of the Folk that exposed themselves, several of the Fire-Men heaped the dry grass and wood at the mouths of the lower tier of caves. Out of these heaps they conjured the monster we feared — *FIRE*. At first, wisps of smoke arose and curled up the cliff. Then I could see the red-tongued flames darting in and out through the wood like tiny snakes. The smoke grew thicker and thicker, at times shrouding the whole face of the cliff. But I was high up and it did not bother me much, though it stung my eyes and I rubbed them with my knuckles.

Old Marrow-Bone was the first to be smoked out. A light fan of air drifted the smoke away at the time so that I saw clearly. He broke out through the smoke, stepping on a burning coal and screaming with the sudden hurt of it, and essayed to climb up the cliff. The arrows showered about him. He came to a pause on a ledge, clutching a knob of rock for support, gasping and sneezing and shaking his head. He swayed back and forth. The feathered ends of a dozen arrows were sticking out of him. He was an old man, and he did not want to die. He swayed wider and wider, his knees giving under him, and as he swayed he wailed most plaintively. His hand released its grip and he lurched outward to the fall. His old bones must have been sadly broken. He groaned and strove feebly to rise, but a Fire-Man rushed in upon him and brained him with a club.

And as it happened with Marrow-Bone, so it happened with many of the Folk. Unable to endure the smoke-suffocation, they rushed out to fall beneath the arrows. Some of the women and children remained in the caves to strangle to death, but the majority met death outside.

When the Fire-Men had in this fashion cleared the first tier of caves, they began making arrangements to duplicate the operation on the second tier of caves. It was while they were climbing up with their grass and wood, that Red-Eye, followed by his wife, with the baby holding to her tightly, made a successful flight up the cliff. The Fire-Men must have concluded that in the interval between the smoking-out operations we would remain in our caves; so that they were unprepared, and their arrows did not begin to fly till Red-Eye and his wife were well up the wall. When he reached the top, he turned about and glared down at them, roaring and beating his chest. They arched their arrows at him, and though he was untouched he fled on.

I watched a third tier smoked out, and a fourth. A few of the Folk escaped up the cliff, but most of them were shot off the face of it as they strove to climb. I remember Long-Lip. He got as far as my ledge, crying piteously, an arrow clear through his chest, the feathered shaft sticking out behind, the bone head sticking out before, shot through the back as he climbed. He sank down on my ledge bleeding profusely at the mouth.

It was about this time that the upper tiers seemed to empty themselves spontaneously. Nearly all the Folk not yet smoked out stampeded up the cliff at the same time. This was the saving of many. The Fire People could not shoot arrows fast enough. They filled the air with arrows, and scores of the stricken Folk came tumbling down; but still there were a few who reached the top and got away.

The impulse of flight was now stronger in me than curiosity. The arrows had ceased flying. The last of the Folk seemed gone, though there may have been a few still hiding in the upper caves. The Swift One and I started to make a scramble for the cliff-top. At sight of us a great cry went up from the Fire People. This was not caused by me, but by the Swift One. They were chattering excitedly and pointing her out to one another. They did not try to shoot her. Not an arrow was discharged. They began calling softly and coaxingly. I stopped and looked down. She was afraid, and whimpered and urged me on. So we went up over the top and plunged into the trees.

This event has often caused me to wonder and speculate. If she were really of their kind, she must have been lost from them at a time when she was too young to remember, else would she not have been afraid of them. On the other hand, it may well have been that while she was their kind she had never been lost from them; that she had been born in the wild forest far from their haunts, her father maybe a renegade Fire-Man, her mother maybe one of my own kind, one of the Folk. But who shall say? These things are beyond me, and the Swift One knew no more about them than did I.

We lived through a day of terror. Most of the survivors fled toward the blueberry swamp and took refuge in the forest in that neighborhood. And all day hunting parties of the Fire People ranged the forest, killing us wherever they found us. It must have been a deliberately executed plan. Increasing beyond the limits of their own territory, they had decided on making a conquest of ours. Sorry the conquest! We had no chance against them. It was slaughter, indiscriminate slaughter, for they spared none, killing old and young, effectively ridding the land of our presence.

It was like the end of the world to us. We fled to the trees as a last refuge, only to be surrounded and killed, family by family. We saw much of this during that day, and besides,

I wanted to see. The Swift One and I never remained long in one tree, and so escaped being surrounded. But there seemed no place to go. The Fire-Men were everywhere, bent on their task of extermination. Every way we turned we encountered them, and because of this we saw much of their handiwork.

I did not see what became of my mother, but I did see the Chatterer shot down out of the old home-tree. And I am afraid that at the sight I did a bit of joyous teetering. Before I leave this portion of my narrative, I must tell of Red-Eye. He was caught with his wife in a tree down by the blueberry swamp. The Swift One and I stopped long enough in our flight to see. The Fire-Men were too intent upon their work to notice us, and, furthermore, we were well screened by the thicket in which we crouched.

Fully a score of the hunters were under the tree, discharging arrows into it. They always picked up their arrows when they fell back to earth. I could not see Red-Eye, but I could hear him howling from somewhere in the tree.

Q

After a short interval his howling grew muffled. He must have crawled into a hollow in the trunk. But his wife did not win this shelter. An arrow brought her to the ground. She was severely hurt, for she made no effort to get away. She crouched in a sheltering way over her baby (which clung tightly to her), and made pleading signs and sounds to the Fire-Men. They gathered about her and laughed at her — even as Lop-Ear and I had laughed at the old Tree-Man. And even as we had poked him with twigs and sticks, so did the Fire-Men with Red-Eye's wife. They poked her with the ends of their bows, and prodded her in the ribs. But she was poor fun. She would not fight. Nor, for that matter, would she get angry. She continued to crouch over her baby and to plead. One of the Fire-Men stepped close to her. In his hand was a club. She saw and understood, but she made only the pleading sounds until the blow fell.

Red-Eye, in the hollow of the trunk, was safe from their arrows. They stood together and debated for a while, then one of them climbed

into the tree. What happened up there I
could not tell, but I heard him yell and saw the
excitement of those that remained beneath.
After several minutes his
body crashed down to
the ground. He did not
move. They looked at him
and raised his head, but it fell
back limply when they let go.
Red-Eye had accounted for
himself.

They were very angry. There
was an opening into the
trunk close to the ground.
They gathered wood and grass
and built a fire. The Swift
One and I, our arms around
each other, waited and watched in the
thicket. Sometimes they threw upon the fire
green branches with many leaves, whereupon
the smoke became very thick.

We saw them suddenly swerve back from the
tree. They were not quick enough. Red-
Eye's flying body landed in the midst of them.

He was in a frightful rage, smashing about with his long arms right and left. He pulled the face off one of them, literally pulled it off with those gnarly fingers of his and those tremendous muscles. He bit another through the neck. The Fire-Men fell back with wild fierce yells, then rushed upon him. He managed to get hold of a club and began crushing heads like eggshells. He was too much for them, and they were compelled to fall back again. This was his chance, and he turned his back upon them and ran for it, still howling wrathfully. A few arrows sped after him, but he plunged into a thicket and was gone.

The Swift One and I crept quietly away, only to run foul of another party of Fire-Men. They chased us into the blueberry swamp, but we knew the tree-paths across the farther morasses where they could not follow on the ground, and so we escaped. We came out on the other side into a narrow strip of forest that separated the blueberry swamp from the great swamp that extended westward. Here we met Lop-Ear. How he had escaped I cannot imagine, unless he had not slept the preceding night at the caves.

Here, in the strip of forest, we might have built tree-shelters and settled down; but the Fire People were performing their work of extermination thoroughly. In the afternoon, Hair-Face and his wife fled out from among the trees to the east, passed us, and were gone. They fled silently and swiftly, with alarm in their faces. In the direction from which they had come we heard the cries and yells of the hunters, and the screeching of some one of the Folk. The Fire People had found their way across the swamp.

The Swift One, Lop-Ear, and I followed on the heels of Hair-Face and his wife. When we came to the edge of the great swamp, we stopped. We did not know its paths. It was outside our territory, and it had been always avoided by the Folk. None had ever gone into it — at least, to return. In our minds it represented mystery and fear, the terrible unknown. As I say, we stopped at the edge of it. We were afraid. The cries of the

Fire-Men were drawing nearer. We looked at one another. Hair-Face ran out on the quaking morass and gained the firmer footing of a grass-hummock a dozen yards away. His

wife did not follow. She tried to, but shrank back from the treacherous surface and cowered down.

The Swift One did not wait for me, nor did she pause till she had passed beyond Hair-Face a hundred yards and gained a much larger hummock. By the time Lop-Ear and I had caught up with her, the Fire-Men appeared among the trees. Hair-Face's wife, driven by them into panic terror, dashed after us. But she ran blindly, without caution, and broke through the crust. We turned and watched, and saw them shoot her with arrows as she sank down in the mud. The arrows began falling about us. Hair-Face had now joined us, and the four of us plunged on, we knew not whither, deeper and deeper into the swamp.

CHAPTER XVIII

OF our wanderings in the great swamp I have no clear knowledge. When I strive to remember, I have a riot of unrelated impressions and a loss of time-value. I have no idea of how long we were in that vast everglade, but it must have been for weeks. My memories of what occurred invariably take the form of nightmare. For untold ages, oppressed by protean fear, I am aware of wandering, endlessly wandering, through a dank and soggy wilderness, where poisonous snakes struck at us, and animals roared around us, and the mud quaked under us and sucked at our heels.

I know that we were turned from our course countless times by streams and lakes and slimy seas. Then there were storms and risings of the water over great areas of the low-lying lands; and there were periods of hunger

"Large trees are about us, and from their branches hang gray
filaments of moss."

and misery when we were kept prisoners in
the trees for days and days by these transient
floods.

Very strong upon me is one picture. Large
trees are about us, and from their branches
hang gray filaments of moss, while great creep-
ers, like monstrous serpents, curl around the
trunks and writhe in tangles through the air.
And all about is the mud, soft mud, that bub-
bles forth gases, and that heaves and sighs
with internal agitations. And in the midst of
all this are a dozen of us. We are lean and
wretched, and our bones show through our
tight-stretched skins. We do not sing and
chatter and laugh. We play no pranks. For
once our volatile and exuberant spirits are
hopelessly subdued. We make plaintive, querulous noises, look at one another, and cluster
close together. It is like the meeting of the
handful of survivors after the day of the end
of the world.

This event is without connection with the
other events in the swamp. How we ever
managed to cross it, I do not know, but at last

we came out where a low range of hills ran down to the bank of the river. It was our river emerging like ourselves from the great swamp. On the south bank, where the river had broken its way through the hills, we found many sand-stone caves. Beyond, toward the west, the ocean boomed on the bar that lay across the river's mouth. And here, in the caves, we settled down in our abiding-place by the sea.

There were not many of us. From time to time, as the days went by, more of the Folk appeared. They dragged themselves from the swamp singly, and in twos and threes, more dead than alive, mere perambulating skeletons, until at last there were thirty of us. Then no more came from the swamp, and Red-Eye was not among us. It was noticeable that no children had survived the frightful journey.

I shall not tell in detail of the years we lived by the sea. It was not a happy abiding-place. The air was raw and chill, and we suffered continually from coughing and colds. We could not survive in such an environment. True, we had children; but they had little hold on life and died early, while we died faster than new ones were born. Our number steadily diminished.

Then the radical change in our diet was not good for us. We got few vegetables and fruits, and became fish-eaters. There were mussels and abalones and clams and rock-oysters, and great ocean-crabs that were thrown upon the beaches in stormy weather. Also, we found several kinds of seaweed that were good to eat. But the change in diet caused us stomach troubles, and none of us ever waxed fat. We were all lean and dyspeptic-looking. It was in getting the big abalones that Lop-Ear was lost. One of them closed upon his fingers at low-tide, and then the flood-tide came in and drowned him. We found his body the next day, and it was a lesson to us.

Not another one of us was ever caught in the closing shell of an abalone.

The Swift One and I managed to bring up one child, a boy — at least we managed to bring him along for several years. But I am quite confident he could never have survived that terrible climate. And then, one day, the Fire People appeared again. They had come down the river, not on a catamaran, but in a rude dug-out. There were three of them that paddled in it, and one of them was the little wizened old hunter. They landed on our beach, and he limped across the sand and examined our caves.

They went away in a few minutes, but the Swift One was badly scared. We were all frightened, but none of us to the extent that she was. She whimpered and cried and was restless all that night. In the morning she took the child in her arms, and by sharp cries, gestures, and example, started me on our second long flight. There were eight of the Folk (all that was left of the horde) that remained behind in the caves. There was no hope for them.

Without doubt, even if the Fire People did not return, they must soon have perished. It was a bad climate down there by the sea. The Folk were not constituted for the coast-dwelling life. We travelled south, for days skirting the great swamp but never venturing into it. Once we broke back to the westward, crossing a range of mountains and coming down to the coast. But it was no place for us. There were no trees — only bleak headlands, a thundering surf, and strong winds that seemed never to cease from blowing. We turned back across the mountains, travelling east and south, until we came in touch with the great swamp again.

Soon we gained the southern extremity of the swamp, and we continued our course south and east. It was a pleasant land. The air was warm, and we were again in the forest. Later on we crossed a low-lying range of hills and found ourselves in an even better forest country. The farther we penetrated from the coast the warmer we found it, and we went on and on until we came to a large river that seemed familiar to the Swift One. It was where she must have come during the four years' absence from the horde. This river we crossed on logs, landing on the other side at the base of a large bluff. High up on the bluff we found our new home — a cave most diffi-cult of access and quite hid-den from any eye be-neath.

There is little more of my tale to tell. Here the Swift One and I lived and reared our family. And here my memo-ries end. We never made another migration. I never dream beyond our high, inacces-sible cave. And here born the child that inherited the stuff of my dreams, that had moulded into its being all the impressions of my life — or of the life of Big-Tooth, rather, who is my other-self, and not my real self, but who is so real to me that often I am unable to tell what age I am living in.

I often wonder about this line of descent. I, the modern, am incontestably a man; yet I, Big-Tooth, the primitive, am not a man. Somewhere, and by straight line of descent, these two parties to my dual personality were connected. Were the Folk, before their destruction, in the process of becoming men? And did I and mine carry through this process? On the other hand, may not some descendant of mine have gone in to the Fire People and become one of them? I do not know. There is no way of learning. One thing only is certain, and that is that Big-Tooth did stamp into the cerebral constitution of one of his progeny all the impressions of his life, and stamped them in so indelibly that the hosts of intervening generations have failed to obliterate them.

There is one other thing of which I must speak before I close. It is a dream that I dream often, and in point of time the real event must have occurred during the period of my living in the high, inaccessible cave.

R

I remember that I wandered far in the forest toward the east. There I came upon a tribe of Tree People. I crouched in a thicket and watched them at play. They were holding a laughing council, jumping up and down and screeching rude choruses.

Suddenly they hushed their noise and ceased their capering. They shrank down in fear, and quested anxiously about with their eyes for a way of retreat. Then Red-Eye walked in among them. They cowered away from him. All were frightened. But he made no attempt to hurt them. He was one of them. At his heels, on stringy bended legs, supporting herself with knuckles to the ground on either side, walked an old female of the Tree People, his latest wife. He sat down in the midst of the circle. I can see him now, as I write this, scowling, his eyes inflamed, as he peers about him at the circle of the Tree People. And as he peers he crooks one monstrous leg and with his gnarly toes scratches himself on the stomach. He is Red-Eye, the atavism.

EPILOGUE

JACK LONDON, EVOLUTIONIST

Loren Eiseley

Fifty-five years have passed since *Before Adam* was written. Within that time many men have tried their hands at picturing the lives of our remote ancestors. Most have confined themselves to those later folk whom London called *The Fire People.* In all this long half-century, though our knowledge of human evolution has increased tremendously, it is my belief that no writer has since produced so moving and vivid a picture of man's primordial past as has Jack London.

As a half-grown boy I reveled in the book, opening as it did vast vistas of the human past with which I was unfamiliar. Reading it today as a professional anthropologist, I find that none of that old thrill has departed. Scientific details, it is true, have altered, and for those changes I will shortly account. But there is a strange and wonderful quality about this work upon which no reviewer has ever commented. It is this: Jack London has made the lives of our uttermost ancestors, Big-Tooth, Lop-Ear, the Swift-One, for all their speechless inadequacy, more appealing than those of the true men, the Fire People who destroyed them. It is plain where London's sympathy lies: It rests with the underdog, the arrowless ones, the people who had not acquired the deadly killing nature of

the true men. The great swamp that is the scene
of Big-Tooth's final flight, that waste which caused
my flesh to creep even as a boy, I as a man now
mentally perceive as a symbol of man's long journey, harried by his own ferocity from age to age.

The plot of the book is ingenious but simple.
London has used the three major stages of human evolution as projected by the Darwinian evo-
lutionists of the late nineteenth century: an arboreal stage represented by the Tree People; a
semi-terrestrial "missing link" stage, "The Folk,"
which is composed of Big-Tooth, the hero, and his
kinsmen; and, finally, London introduces nemesis
in the shape of the true men, the Fire People.
These last seem intended to equate roughly with
that stage of culture which archaeologists of to-
day would call the Upper Paleolithic, the period
extending roughly from 30,000 to 8,000 B.C., although the bow and arrow were introduced later.
Red-Eye, the atavism, is intended to suggest some
ferocious gorilloid throwback to a time even more
remote than that represented by the living Tree
People of the book.

By thus overlapping these three human stages
in time, London succeeds in not only introducing
more action into his pages, but indirectly giving
the reader a more extended glimpse of our evolutionary tree. The selection of one stage alone to
write about would not have been nearly so effective as this conflict between men, some of whom
were already living fossils on the verge of extinction, as in the case of the Folk. The question the
modern reader will want to ask at this point is
just how much of this story is valid today. The

number of human fossils known when London wrote his book were few. Much of what was theorized about human evolution was based solely upon our knowledge of the habits of the existing great apes who were presumed to be roughly similar to the tree stage of our own remote ancestors. Some of this coloration is to be found in London's book. If it is not now entirely acceptable, one must remember it was proper scientific theory in London's own time.

In honesty it has to be pointed out that we now know with great certainty the following facts:

1. The human evolutionary tree cannot be telescoped in time sufficiently to make all these human stages overlap in a way that was conceivable in the late Darwinian epoch. Later information indicates that the age of the world implies a far longer human history than was assumed early in our century before we had learned to clock geological time by the radioactive decay of elements in the rocks.

2. Discoveries, buttressed particularly by finds in the post-war years, have revealed that ape-men, on about the level of intellect portrayed by "The Folk" of London's story, were not semi-arboreal but were already completely bipedal, walking on two legs, although still massive jawed, short-faced "apes." These creatures did not possess the large canine teeth visualized by the early Darwinists on the basis of erroneous comparisons of early man with the anatomical peculiarities of the living great apes. Moreover, there is considerable evidence that they were already very primitive tool users, although they appear to have lacked the

use of fire. Whether they had achieved an incipient speech level may be suspected but is not demonstrable, since much of their meager cultural activity might have been transferred from one generation to another by pure imitation. Unfortunately, there are decided limits to what the physical remains of the half-men can reveal to us about the nature of the dawning human consciousness.

3. The result of these discoveries suggests that the nineteenth-century scholars upon whom Jack London relied for his factual materials were so hypnotized by our living relatives, the great apes, that they failed utterly to anticipate man might have entered the grassland environment of the early planet at a far earlier time—that he had been, in fact, a successful ground-dwelling, erect-walking ape long before he had undergone those final cranial changes that had left him a man. Only the great contemporary of the English evolutionist Charles Darwin (1809–1882), the English naturalist Alfred Russel Wallace, caught a glimpse of this possibility, but his ideas, expressed without fossils as evidence, received scant attention in his own time. Rather than seeing foot and brain as altering together, he postulated what we now know to be true: namely, that man's foot had become fully adapted for a terrestrial existence at a different stage, and, seemingly, long before the emergence of the great brain with the final changes that it introduced in the human countenance.

4. These later discovered facts, based on the fossil record, reveal that man early reached the ground from his arboreal apprenticeship in the forest attic. There is no indication that he ever

passed through such a gorilla-like phase as the formidable Red-Eye of London's narrative implies. Rather, man seems to have descended upon the ground at a time when he was smaller than man of today. Perhaps he was still primitive and generalized enough, even as an arboreal creature, that, like the living but archaic gibbon, his weight did not force him back into the pronograde four-footed posture of the living gorilla who can stand, but is more at ease when he has toppled forward upon his massive forelimbs.

5. The fossil record, in the light of the facts we have just narrated, suggests that our first attempts to understand our past have actually been handicapped by too great a concentration upon our living but divergent relatives in the trees. Our path and theirs is now believed to have diverged so long ago that the common ancestor was probably a lithe, light-bodied generalized primate, a member of that mammal order including man, the ape, and the monkey, more monkey-like in size and certain other characteristics than either existing man or the huge-bodied forest anthropoids of our own times. Instead of looking upon these latter as some kind of surviving fossil ancestors, we should rather visualize their great bodies, elongated arms, and short legs as an adaptation for another environment: that is, "walking" by the arms across the forest ceiling, even though, in the case of the chimpanzee and gorilla, there has been a late inadequate venture upon the ground. The existing apes and man, in other words, are both specialized for particular, if divergent, environments.

The great anthropoids, no more than ourselves, are primitive in an evolutionary sense. They belong in our own time as relatives, not ancestral models. Their great jaws and protrusive muzzles are a specialized vegetarian adaptation to the forest and bush. They are an evolutionary line now coming to its end, as the forest areas of the earth grow ever more circumscribed under human dominance. Anthropoid anatomy and psychology tell us much, but that they reveal the full secret of the human past, that the apes are "living fossils" in a human sense, we no longer believe. He who sees his forebears in the great jaws and massive five-hundred pound body of a gorilla is seeing what has never existed, even though a half-human aura lingers pathetically around these mighty, unfortunate beasts who are doomed to early extinction.

Realizing the extent to which evolutionary thought has changed in fifty years of discovery, the reader may wish to ask what is the value, outside of a well-written narrative for an off hour, that this book still presents. What, I ask myself, is its remaining significance—this old book of my childhood which I fondle so affectionately and which long ago unconsciously set me on the path of my profession.

As a historian of science I could say it presents a vivid picture of anthropological thinking around the turn of the century, but I would be merely defending, on a needlessly academic level, a book which needs no defense. If London telescoped time with his juxtaposition of the Tree People, the Folk, and the Fire People, we would still have to admit that the human story, even as known archae-

ologically, permits the assumption that by middle-
Ice Age times more than one human type was still
in existence and, indeed, that what the paleon-
tologist would call "structural ancestors"—that is,
living fossils—also survived. In fact, it is gener-
ally conceded that the last of the grassland apes
may have been struck down by the first
paleanthropic men—the forerunners of modern
man—who had been derived at some earlier point
from these same forms.

The grass world is a different world than that
of the trees. In the arboreal domain there are
many levels, many environmental niches in which
diverse forms of primates, whether archaic or advanced, can specialize and survive without coming into conflict. Old-fashioned lemurs, monkeys,
and great apes have survived side by side. In the
one-dimensional world of the grass such competi-
tors as diverse upright bipedal apes could not long
survive. As London hints, in his story of the Swift
One, both miscegenation and extermination
played their role. In the end that creature now
known among us as *Homo sapiens,* ourselves, was
the victor. On the grass which provided the first
great game supplies for man the hunter, all of our
forerunners, our lost relatives, have vanished. Perhaps—who knows—we are in the end less the vic-
tors than the destroyers. Perhaps this is why the
Fire People, an early version of our own kind,
move through London's pages as a spreading piti-
less horror disturbing the ancient balance of nature. Perhaps for a moment we wish to return from
our mid-century world of terror to be among the
Folk at the drinking place, to be simple, wordless,

and childlike even amidst the dangers of that vanished world.

Then, too, London does not demean these remote ancestors of ours. He perceives in them the first signs of those strange loyalties, in love, in human relations, which have been so badly maligned within our time. For all the harshness of this world, pictured in the grimmest terms, there lingers across it the air of some indescribable nostalgic autumn. Was it worth it to become man, one wonders, traversing in memory, like Big-Tooth's descendant, the landscape of that remote and fearsome age?

Here Saber-Tooth pads along the path to the drinking place; snakes strike at our naked feet; around us are the barriers of great swamps, unknown rivers or cold and naked shores. Yet, I who in childhood was so entranced with this country that I dreamed of it, like Big-Tooth's modern descendant who tells the story, am still loath to leave this land far gone in time. The sadness of time past had not then overtaken our happy youthfulness; the Fire People had not yet totally appropriated our caves or hunted us out of existence. No, good people who read this book, I am as I was in youth, one of the Folk. If I live on among you, it is in disguise. That autumnal country through which Big-Tooth and the Swift One made their way on their last flight from man is still my country, even if I am forced to seek for it a little farther down in time than London imagined or even if a few anachronisms have to be ignored or a few bits of anatomy altered with the changing times.

It is there I came to an understanding of the

thing that I once was, and I remain not too sure that I am satisfied about the inevitable victory of the Fire People. All my adult life I have continued the flight through that vast swampland which has become for me the symbol of man's displacement from his natural home in nature. If there is no longer Red-Eye, the atavism, there is occasionally among us a hidden remnant of the Folk. It is this that creates the everlasting quality of *Before Adam*. The more perceptive among us turn its pages and by some haunting, inescapable compulsion find that we are not the Fire People at all. We are, for all our modern skins, the lost, eternally lost, but still safe-hidden remnant of the Folk. Lop-Ear lives on among us and, in the world of childhood, the haze across that country becomes so tenuous that every now and then one of us breaks through it so successfully that he lives out his secret life there—just as did Big-Tooth and his love, the Swift One, in their lone and last high cave.

LISTING OF PEOPLES AND CHARACTERS

I. THE PEOPLES OF THE YOUNGER WORLD

Fire People

The most physically and culturally advanced of the Younger World humanoid species, the Fire People most closely resemble modern humans. They are the least hairy, have smaller heads, are less stooped, have shorter arms, and possess smaller, less fanglike teeth than the Folk and the Tree People. The Fire People wear clothes (animal skins worn around the waist and across the shoulders), use the bow and arrow to deadly effect, communicate through a fully developed language, are masters of fire, and are well organized and adept at cooperation to achieve goals. They do not domesticate animals. The men are proficient hunters of animals and other humanoid species, normally hunting in groups of two or three. The Fire People, like the Folk, prefer to live in cave shelters. At the beginning of the story, they make their home to the northeast of the Folk and, due to their prosperity, are expanding their hunting territory and habitations into the homeland of the Folk.

The Folk

The humanoid species occupying the middle rung of the evolutionary ladder in the Younger World, the Folk are more physically and culturally advanced than the Tree People but less so than the Fire People. They have less hair than the apes and Tree People—and pride themselves on that attribute—and shorter arms and thicker legs, yet they remain very adept at climbing and grasping with their feet. They engage in rudimentary communication, in the form of pantomime and a vocabulary of thirty to forty sounds, and do use some tools, including sticks and stones for weapons and gourds for carrying water and foodstuffs. They are omnivores, eating all types of small game, eggs, fish, carrots, and hazelnuts. The Folk are in the midst of evolving from living in trees to living on the ground; consequently, while most live in natural caves in cliffs along a river, some still make their homes in trees in a nearby forest. The tree-dwellers live in crude, wooden shelters that are roofed. Those who make their homes in caves avoid living in the larger caves near the ground that are more vulnerable to predators. Most Folk die from violence and few make it to middle age. The Folk have a fluid social organization. Monogamy is infrequently practiced; leadership is by brute force rather than consensus; with the exception of the "hee-hee councils" (a spontaneous, emotional eruption of beaten and vocalized rhythms) there is little coordination or planning among the group as a whole. The Folk are not good fighters but survive by being "cunning and cowardly," running away and hiding at the first opportunity. They are known for their curiosity, mockery, excessive and often cruel humor, and lack of foresight and purpose.

Tree People

The least advanced of the humanoid species, the Tree People resemble apes but have no hair on their faces, palms, or soles. These forest-dwellers live in groups, use sounds like those of the Folk to communicate, and are hostile to outsiders. They move slower on foot than the Folk but can outdistance them in the trees. They do congregate for a "laughing council"; this meeting, though mentioned, is not described in detail in the story.

II. THE FOLK

Big-Face

A mature, rather large male who keeps his temper less in check around Red-Eye than most other Folk.

Big-Tooth

The protagonist of the story and a remote ancestor of the narrator, a twentieth-century California man who is linked to Big-Tooth through racial memories in the form of vivid dreams. Big-Tooth has "pronouncedly large" eyeteeth. Although born in a crude tree shelter, Big Tooth was at a young age driven from his home by his stepfather, the Chatterer, and soon joined the Folk living in caves. He has two siblings (one is a sister), a mate (the Swift One), and, eventually, a son.

Broken-Tooth

A young member of the cave-dwelling Folk who
was evicted from his birth cave by his mother and
took up residence with Big-Tooth and Lop-Ear.
Broken-Tooth is very agile and skilled at playing
tag in the trees.

Chatterer

The mate of Big-Tooth's mother after his father
was killed. The Chatterer is a schemer who takes
delight in talking and malicious pranks. He drove
his stepson, Big-Tooth, from his tree home.

Crooked-Leg

A quiet, small male who is the mate of the Singing One.

Hair Face

An adult male who appears briefly late in the story
when he joins Big-Tooth, Lop-Ear, and the Swift
One on an epic, desperate trip across a swamp.

Hairless One

The son of the ancient Marrow-Bone, who shares
a cave with his father and mate. He has a son
(Long Lip) and daughter (the Singing One).

Long Lip

The son of the Hairless One and grandson of
Marrow-Bone. One of his chief tasks is to carry
water in a gourd for his grandfather.

Lop-Ear

The male friend and constant companion of Big-Tooth, named because one of his ears is droopy. Lop-Ear is a year older than Big-Tooth and probably an orphan. He briefly took Big-Tooth's sister as a mate. Lop-Ear is in general more inventive than Big-Tooth and remains at his side throughout the story.

Marrow-Bone

A very old member of the Folk (a rarity) who moves slowly and boasts a "bit of a sparse and straggly white beard." He lives in a cave with his son (the Hairless One) and has grandchildren (Long-Lip and the Singing One). Marrow-Bone is quite sickly, often staying in his cave and needing water to be brought to him by his grandson. He is apparently respected by all of the Folk; even the ferocious Red-Eye does not strike him, even when he has the opportunity.

Red-Eye

Named for his perpetually inflamed, red-rimmed eyes, he is the de facto leader of the Folk, dominating them by terror and brute strength. Red-Eye is a throwback to a more primitive humanoid species than the Folk; he weighs one hundred seventy pounds, is enormously large and strong, can spring twenty feet from a sitting position, and will sometimes knuckle-walk like apes. He kills many Folk to get their mates and then ends up killing the mates in fits of temper.

Singing One

The daughter of the Hairless One and granddaughter of Marrow-Bone. She is known for singing at the mouth of the cave during dusk. Her mate is Crooked-Leg.

Swift One

A female friend and later mate of Big-Tooth, she is evidently one of the Fire People or closely related to them. The narrator observes that her incisors are less pronounced, her nose less squat, and her countenance more mild than female Folk. The Swift One is known for her agility, timidity, and fear of lightning.

REVIEWS OF THE FIRST EDITION

FROM THE *ATLANTIC MONTHLY*

In the subject of his latest story, *Before Adam,* Mr. Jack London shows no diminution of his characteristic audacity. The hero is an ape-man of the Mid-Pleistocene period, by name Big-Tooth, who through the mouth of his latter-day descendant tells of his life among the Tree Folk and the Cave Folk and the Fire People.

That life was not destitute of adventure. One of his earliest memories is of being rescued by his mother—"she was like a large orang-utan, my mother, or like a chimpanzee, and yet, in sharp and definite ways, quite different"—from the ravenous tusks of a wild boar that has come upon him in the fern-brake. Clutching her with hand and foot he was borne to safety in the tree overhead. Some years later, as soon as his age permitted, he was cast forth to shift for himself. He joined the community of the Cave Folk. He foraged for roots and eggs and berries. He lived in terror of darkness and snakes, of Red-Eye,—who it seems "was an atavism,"—and of the mysterious Northeast whence appeared the smoke of the Fire People. He went on a journey with Lop-Ear, his cave-mate, through strange morasses and along

Harry James Smith, "Some Recent Novels," review in *Atlantic Monthly,* July 1907, 125–27.

unknown rivers, and finally, after an ardent if simple courtship, he was united to Swift One.

Perhaps the most provocative passage in the book is that which describes the devotion of Lop-Ear to his comrade at a moment of danger. Big-Tooth had been pierced below the knee by one of the arrows of the murderous Fire People, and his flight was cruelly impeded.

Once again Lop-Ear tried to drag the arrow through the flesh, and I angrily stopped him. Then he bent down and began gnawing the shaft of the arrow with his teeth. . . . I often meditate upon this scene—the two of us, half-grown cubs, in the childhood of the race, and the one mastering his fear, beating down his selfish impulse of flight, in order to stand by and succor the other. And there rises up before me all that was there foreshadowed, and I see visions of Damon and Pythias, of life-saving crews and Red Cross nurses, of martyrs and leaders of forlorn hopes, of Father Damien, and of the Christ himself, and of all the men of earth, mighty of stature, whose strength may trace back to the elemental loins of Lop-Ear and Big-Tooth and other denizens of the Younger World.

This is a brave endeavor to enlist our interest in these dim denizens; but it falls short of complete success. The story occasionally stirs our curiosity, but never our sympathy. We shudder a little before the exhibitions of Red-Eye's ferocity, much as we might in visiting a shambles; we admire the ingenuity and plausibility of Mr. London's psychology, his capacity for realizing primitive states of mind; but farther we do not go.

It may be that the very nature of his effort precludes this. The imaginative process in the present instance has not been that of investing brute life with human attributes, but that of divesting humanity of its human attributes. In interesting us in wolf-dogs and B'rer Rabbits Uncle Remus and Jack London have followed essentially the same process: they have made them seem human. They have brought them into the pale of affinity, given them a psychology in which we may share. But in the present instance the differences must be emphasized all the time rather than the likenesses. It may be possible to see in the fidelity of Lop-Ear a foreglimpse of life-saving crews and Red Cross nurses; but such telescopic vision does not greatly stir the heart. The affair of Big-Tooth and Swift One is the inversion of romance. The most valued products of life are not greatly valued in their origins: the rudiments may have technical or scientific interest, and the author would doubtless claim some special merit for his story upon the score of scientific plausibility; but that is obviously a matter apart.

Mr. London's story is simply one further step—one could hope the last—in the development of a type of fiction with which of late we have been adequately supplied. It would be interesting to examine the publishers' announcements of the last two or three years with a view to computing the frequency of such phrases as "life drunk to the dregs,"—"strong, primitive emotions,"—"thrilling with fierce passion and the heat of it,"—"human nature stripped naked, by salt water alchemy reduced to its rudiments"—whatever that may mean. The thing that impresses one most forcibly after perusing a successive half-dozen of these "red-blooded" novels (it seems superfluous to name them) is the sheer vulgarity of them, or perhaps, more definitively, their materiality. In them passion is no longer a fire for the annealing or fusing of character; it seems to have become an object in itself, hardly to be distinguished from appetite. The promoters of the type, in a noisy effort to get at "realities," have flung away the choicest and most significant of life's possessions, and the realities are discovered to be little more than raw sensations.

With the elimination of each subtler and more spiritual ingredient, personality is stripped of its distinctions. Men's bodies do not greatly differ from one another; neither do their elemental emotions. As we go downward the field is restricted instead of enlarged, for we have sacrificed what is of chiefest importance in fiction: the individual. Lop-Ear and Big-Tooth are practically interchangeable, save for the mere accidents of physique which denominate them; and the love of Swift One signifies little, as it is only the crude satisfaction of an instinct. And since the repetition of a raw sensation soon palls, if it does not become actually painful, the use of the primitive for its own sake—just because it is "red-blooded"— is sure to involve its own defeat.

Fortunately this is not the only end to which the primitive may be used. True though it be that elemental character lacks a degree of sharpness and individuality, it is also true that, seen in its relations, it often gains a certain largeness and dignity which are impressive. In looking at the sower at nightfall, Victor Hugo saw his shadow extending mysteriously across the face of the world. Millet felt that reverence too, and imbued humble things with the same augustness. Our modern approach to nature is one which especially favors this use of the primitive subject. To the poets and romancers of an earlier generation Nature was a benignant friend, clad in beauty and goodness; she was man's best teacher in high things. The moralistic and decorative uses of nature were chiefly emphasized. But with the triumph of evolutionary philosophy the shores were struck from under this conception. Parasite and host were seen to be produced by the self-same process; there was no distinction in nature between good and bad; there was no mercy, no benevolence. Irresistibly and irrevocably the activities of life were borne forward; types appeared, struggled, disappeared, were forgotten. The whole process in its first shock upon the imagination seemed cruelly impersonal. Reverence had been attacked in her very temple; it was gloomily predicted that the scalpel of science would bring death to imagination.

Undeniably the old gods are gone; and it can hardly be asserted that we are as yet fully assured of the new. But imagination is too integral a human function to be eradicated by a change in philosophy. The nature-worshiping instinct holds its place in the heart against all comers; only it expresses itself in different forms. One means, and perhaps the most promising, by which nature has been reclaimed and revitalized for the imagination is through the recognition of its genetic relationship with all life. We are also her offspring. Our landscape setting, our social environment (the notion of "nature" must be extended beyond fauna and flora and rurality), has a vital role in the drama; is no longer a mere moral for it, or a pictured curtain let down behind it and removable at will. This interplay of personal and extra-personal forces is most apprehensible of course where neither "environment" nor "individual" is over-complex. A simple personality is in more clearly perceptible ways the product of its circumstances—akin to them—than a highly-developed personality. In this fact lies, I think, much of the characteristically modern appeal which the primitive in human life makes to the poetic imagination.

FROM THE *NEW YORK TIMES*

This most singular stretch of imagination impresses one first as almost absurd, then as fantastic, then as interesting, and finally as a remarkable achievement. That is to say, the conception of a narrative based on the life and adventures of a prehistoric cave dweller, half man and half ape, is so dumfounding as not to be readily grasped. As the reader progresses the vitality and realism of the story beget a fascination which ultimately reaches conviction. In a general sense, though purely a work of fiction and tinged with no devitalizing touch of scientific investigation, *Before*

"Jack London's Idea of Primitive Man," review in the *New York Times*, 9 March 1907, 145.

Adam must be a most disconcerting book for those of our brothers and sisters who feel that it would be improper or irreligious to believe in our descent from "arboreal ancestors."

The story is introduced through the medium of dreams—strange, atavistic nightmares which have been the terror of the author's childhood. Though reared in the city, he has dreamed of forests, caves, and all the terrible creatures of the wilderness. He has seen himself as one of a mysterious tribe of beings—savage, hairy, and naked. His dreams have been incoherent and without any sense of time, yet vivid and oft repeated. In his maturity he has come to understand the significance of these nightly horrors, to interpret them as inherent reversions of the long-buried past, to classify them and arrange them in intelligible progression.

The author, or rather the creature in whose existence the author recollects his own former life, is naturally the hero of the book. In the dreams, the creatures had no names, for they lived in the era when the nearest approach to language was some score of broken calls and sounds, but in the narrative, for the sake of convenience, they have all been christened. The hero is Big-Tooth, his bosom friend and comrade is Lop-Ear, his obnoxious step-father is the Chatterer, the female with whom he finally mates is the Swift One, and the giant arch-fiend of the tribe is Red-Eye. These characters, together with Big-Tooth's mother and sister, are the leading dramatis personnae of the entire history.

His first remembrance of himself is as an infant in a nest in the trees, and his first adventure comes when, left on the ground, his mother rescues him from a wild boar, and, with him clinging tightly to her hairy chest, swings again high up into the branches. His mother is "old fashioned" and remains in the trees, but most of the members of the tribe live in the caves, whither he goes when driven from home by the tyranny of the Chatterer. The tribe is superior to the Tree People, the apes, but inferior to the terrible Fire People, the barbaric race of elemental men who have discovered fire and the use of bows and arrows. Lop-Ear and Big-Tooth make a long journey, full of adventures. The Fire People drive the tribe from their caves and those who are not slain wander again into the forests. Finally Big-Tooth and the Swift One settle and rear a family in an unknown land.

Jack London has performed a wonderful feat in so describing the lives and passions of these rudimentary beings. He has builded a romance of the unknown ages, of the creatures that may have been, and endowed it all with poignant reality.

IN THE BISON FRONTIERS OF
IMAGINATION SERIES

The Wonder
By J. D. Beresford
Introduced by Jack L. Chalker

At the Earth's Core
By Edgar Rice Burroughs
Introduced by Gregory A. Benford
Afterword by Phillip R. Burger

The Land that Time Forgot
By Edgar Rice Burroughs
Introduced by Mike Resnick

Omega: The Last Days of the World
By Camille Flammarion
Introduced by Robert Silverberg

Mizora: A World of Women
By Mary E. Bradley Lane
Introduced by Joan Saberhagen

Before Adam
By Jack London
Introduced by Dennis L. McKiernan

Fantastic Tales
By Jack London
Edited by Dale L. Walker

The Chase of the Golden Meteor
By Jules Verne
Introduced by Gregory A. Benford

When Worlds Collide
By Philip Wylie and Edwin Balmer
Introduced by John Varley

LaVergne, TN USA
14 September 2010
197024LV00006B/121/P